The Right way to French in 39 Steps

Joseph Rosenberg

Contents

Part One

FRENCH-ENGLISH

5

Part Two

ENGLISH-FRENCH

PREFACE

THIS book is intended to give a practical knowledge of the conversational language and especially to enable visitors to French-speaking countries to express their everyday requirements.

The correct use of a foreign language is a habit rather than a knowledge. A person knowing all the rules of French grammar would still be unable to speak the language. The simplest way to learn to speak a foreign language is to memorize the most useful words and expressions, to repeat them again and again until they are on the tip of your tongue whenever you require to use them.

The first part of the book gives you the most useful words and sentences which you must know for whatever purposes you may be learning the language. They have been arranged by an experienced language teacher in such a way that they can be easily memorized. *Learn them by heart through constant repetition.*

The second part gives classified lists of useful vocabulary. Words closely related in sense have been grouped together, under convenient headings, which enable easy reference. The grouping of words in a logical rather than an alphabetical order has been found more suitable for beginners, as it is easier to learn words that are related in sense.

The words given in the second part need not be learned by heart. They can be looked up when required and combined with the set-phrases given in Part I. Thus the student who has memorized the French for " I should like to . . .", " Would you like to . . . ? ", " Where can I find . . . ? ", " Please show me . . .", etc. etc., has a stock of correct language forms at his command which he can enlarge as the occasion arises by picking up suitable words from the lists provided in the second part of the book. He can further extend his vocabulary by the use of a good dictionary.

TABLE OF IMITATED PRONUNCIATION

(Unless given below, same as in English)

ah	like the " a " in " father "
ai	as in " pair "
(*ai*)	the same with rounded lips
ay	as in " tray "
(*ay*)	the same with rounded lips
ee	as in " see "
(*ee*)	the same with rounded lips
e	as in " open "
o	as in " not "
oh	as in " note "
aN	nasal " ah "
oN	nasal " o "
aiN or *iN*	nasal " ai "
(*ai*)N or *uN*	nasal " (ai) "
g	as in " go "
s	as in " so "
y	as in " yes "
zh	like the " s " in " measure "

(Further information in Appendix I)

LE CONGRÈS DU PARTI SOCIALISTE

Les difficultés de l'industrie du cinéma français

LES CRÉDITS SUPPLÉMENTAIRES POUR LA DÉFENSE NATIONALE

Deux nouvelles expéditions au Pôle Nord

UNE PRINCESSE ÉPOUSE UN CHAUFFEUR

HERE are five headlines taken from French newspapers. Even if you have no knowledge of French at all it will not be difficult to recognize these sentences as meaning:

1. The Congress of the Socialist Party.
2. The Difficulties of the French Cinema Industry.
3. Supplementary Credits for National Defence.
4. Two New Expeditions to the North Pole.
5. A Princess Marries a Chauffeur.

Many French words are similar to English words, and it is sometimes possible—with a little guesswork—to make out the sense of many words and sentences in French books or newspapers. If you were reading them to a Frenchman, or a Frenchman reading them out to you, there would be complete bewilder-

ment—neither understanding a word the other was saying. This
is because, although the spelling of words is sometimes alike or
similar, their pronunciation is completely different in the two
languages.

Let us examine these headlines one by one.

LE CONGRÈS DU PARTI SOCIALISTE

le (= the) is pronounced like the italicized part of the word
mil*er*, that is to say, the " e " is just a faint sound, such as you
get in the words " hatter," " baker," " bitter," and it should be
uttered as rapidly as possible.

congrès. The first syllable is very much like " cong " in the
English word " congress," but the French make it a nasal sound,
i.e. as much air as possible must escape through the nose and the
" ng " must not be sounded at all. In our system of imitated pronunciation the nasal sound is indicated by a capital " N." It
is not really a consonant, but merely an indication that the preceding vowel is a nasal.

The second syllable of the word " congrès " is pronounced like
the italicized part of the English word " *grai*n." French " è "
is always pronounced like English " ai " (as in " pair "), and the
final " s," like most final consonants, is not sounded at all. In
our imitated pronunciation we therefore show the word " congrès "
as *koN-grai.*

du (= of the) has a vowel sound which has no English counterpart. It is not difficult to acquire. If you say " dee " with your
lips protruded as if you were going to whistle, you will get the
right sound. As the French " u " is nothing but " ee " said with
rounded lips, we describe this sound in our imitated pronunciation
as (*ee*), indicating by the brackets that the lips have to be
rounded while saying " ee."

parti (= party) is sounded like *pahr-tee*, with equal stress on
both syllables.

socialiste is pronounced *soh-see-ah-leest*, with equal stress on
each of the four syllables.

Les Difficultés de l'Industrie du Cinéma Français

les (= the, plural) is pronounced as *lay*.

difficultés as if it were spelt *dee-fee-k(ee)l-tay*, with equal stress on each syllable. Remember that *(ee)* is " ee " with rounded lips.

de (= of), like the italicized part of " har*de*r."

l'industrie. The first syllable of this word contains another nasal sound. It is very similar to the italicized part of the word " *lan*guage," but again with more breath escaping through the nose and without sounding the " ng " at all. This nasal sound is the nasal counterpart to the " ai " sound described above. It is rendered in our imitated pronunciation as *aiN*. The " du " part of " industrie " is as described above, and French " ie " is sounded as in English " f*ie*ld," so that the whole word can be transcribed as *laiN-d(ee)s-tree*.

du as shown previously.

cinéma is pronounced like *see-nay-mah*, with equal stress on each of the three syllables.

français [*fraN-sai*] brings us to another nasal sound. Its nearest English counterpart would be the vowel heard in the English word " frump," but again with as much air as you can let escape through the nose. It is the same sound as heard at the end of the French word " restaurant," which is pronounced *rais-toh-raN*.

Les Crédits Supplémentaires pour la Défense Nationale

les (plural " the ") is pronounced as *lay*.

crédits sounds like *cray-dee*.

supplémentaires is pronounced *s(ee)p-lay-maN-tair*, i.e. *seep* with lips protruded, *maN* with the nasal " a " as in " français," " restaurant," etc. ; *tair* is sounded very much like the English word " tare."

pour (= for) is pronounced *poor* (but not *poo-er*), the " r " following a pure " oo " sound.

la as in English " *la*st."

défense should be pronounced as *day-faNs*.

nationale is pronounced *nahs-yon-nahl* (say *nas* as in " *nasty*,"
yon as in " *yon*der," *al* as in " chor*ale* ").

DEUX NOUVELLES EXPÉDITIONS AU PÔLE NORD

deux (= two). This word contains another vowel sound for
which there exists no English counterpart. If you say " day "
with your lips rounded, the resulting sound will be the correct
pronunciation of the French word " deux." The final " x " is
not sounded. Similarly, if you say " blay " with rounded lips,
you get the French word " bleu," which means " blue." In our
imitated pronunciation we indicate this sound by (*ay*).

nouvelles (= new) is pronounced *noo-vel*, the *el* as in " *el*m."

expéditions sounds like *aiks-pay-dees-yoN*, with equal stress
on all four syllables.

au (= to the) is pronounced like " oh ! "

Pôle Nord (= North Pole), say *pol* as in " *pol*ice," followed
by *nor* as in " *Nor*wich."

UNE PRINCESSE ÉPOUSE UN CHAUFFEUR

une (= a, feminine) is pronounced (*ee*)*n*, the " ee " with
rounded lips as explained above.

princesse. The first syllable of " princesse " sounds like the
English word " *prank*," not sounding the " k." The second
syllable is pronounced the same as in the English word " prin-
cess."

épouse (= marries) is pronounced *ay-pooz* and rhymes with
" whose."

un chauffeur [(*ai*)*N shoh-f*(*ai*)*r*] (= a chauffeur). The first part
of the word " chauffeur " is pronounced as in English, i.e. like
the word " show." The second syllable is very similar to the
English word " fir." The difference between the English and the
French pronunciation is that in English you stress the first
syllable and mumble the second. In the French pronunciation
of the word both syllables get equal stress : " show-fir."

The " un " brings us to the last of the four nasal sounds. It is the nasal counterpart to the " ir " sound just described. Try to pass as much air as you can through your nose while making the vowel sound of English her, sir or fur.

In our imitated pronunciation we describe the " ir " sound by (*ai*), because it is the " ai " sound (as in " pair ") pronounced with rounded lips. If you say " pair " with rounded lips you get the correct pronunciation of the French word " peur " which means " fear." Its nasal counterpart, which you encounter in such words as parfum, Verdun, lundi (= Monday), etc., is shown as (*ai*)*N*.

The sentences given here should be studied very carefully, as they contain all the French sounds that have no counterparts in English. They are (*ee*), (*ay*) and (*ai*), which are *ee*, *ay* and *ai* pronounced with rounded lips, as well as the four nasals which in our system of imitated pronunciation are rendered by *aN*, *aiN*, *oN* and (*ai*)*N*.

To speak French correctly, it is not enough to know how to pronounce the French sounds. Stress and intonation are also entirely different from English. The most important differences are :

1. All the syllables of French words are evenly pronounced with a slight stress on the last syllable. For instance, in the word **britannique**, which is pronounced *bree-tah-neek*, the pitch of the voice is raised at the end.

2. French is spoken with more emphasis than English, the lips and the tongue are more mobile, and there must be no mumbling or slurring together of syllables. Take, for instance, the word " national," which is common to both languages. It is a word of three syllables, but in colloquial English it is reduced to one : " nashnl." In the French word all three syllables are fully pronounced : *nahs-yoh-nahl.*

SOME NOTES ON FRENCH GRAMMAR

Masculine and Feminine

In French, the names of things as well as the names of persons are either masculine or feminine, and they are referred to as either " he " or " she."

	Masculine			*Feminine*	
le père	*le pair*	the father	**la mère**	*lah mair*	the mother
le frère	*le frair*	the brother	**la sœur**	*lah s(ai)r*	the sister
le livre	*le leevr*	the book	**la table**	*lah tahbl*	the table
le col	*le kol*	the tie	**la manche**	*lah maNsh*	the sleeve

The word for " the " in French is *le* before a masculine noun and *la* before a feminine. There are some practical rules for knowing which nouns are masculine and which are feminine. They will be found on page 122. As these rules do not cover all nouns, the best way is always to learn the noun together with the Definite Article (*le* or *la*).

He and She

le père ; il est grand	*le pair ; ee-lai graN*	the father ; he is tall
la mère ; elle est grande	*lah mair ai-lai graNd*	the mother ; she is tall
le fils ; il est petit	*le fees ; ee-lai p'tee*	the son ; he is small
la fille ; elle est petite	*lah feey ; ai-lai p'teet*	the daughter ; she is small

Note from the above examples that adjectives have masculine and feminine forms.   To obtain the feminine form of an adjective " e " is added to the masculine.   This " e " is mute, but it causes a final consonant to be sounded.   Compare the following :

	Masculine			*Feminine*	
vert	*vair*		**verte**	*vairt*	green
brun	*br(ai)N*		**brune**	*br(ee)n*	brown
rouge	*roozh*		**rouge**	*roozh*	red

joli	*zho-lee*		jolie	*zho-lee*	pretty
beau	*boh*		belle	*bail*	beautiful
bon	*boN*		bonne	*bon*	good
blanc	*blaN*		blanche	*blaNsh*	white

Note.—1. Adjectives ending in "e" have the same form, whether they are masculine or feminine.

2. Adjectives ending in a vowel (other than mute "e") add "e" for the feminine. This, however, does not affect their pronunciation.

3. Some adjectives have more or less irregular feminine forms.

Singular and Plural

le mur *le m(ee)r* the wall

la porte *lah port* the door

l'enfant *laN-faN* the child.

le Français *le fraN-sai* the Frenchman

la Française *lah fraN-saiz* the Frenchwoman

l'Anglais *laN-glai* the Englishman

l'Anglaise *laN-glaiz* the Englishwoman

le petit garçon *le p'tee gahr-soN* the little boy

la petite fille *lah p'teet feey* the little girl

les murs *lay m(ee)r* the walls

les portes *lay port* the doors

les enfants *lay-zaN-faN* the children

les Français *lay fraN-sai* the Frenchmen ; the French

les Françaises *lay fraN-saiz* the Frenchwomen

les Anglais *lay-zaN-glai* the Englishmen ; the English

les Anglaises *lay-zaN-glaiz* the Englishwomen

les petits garçons *lay p'tee gahr-soN* the little boys

les petites filles *lay p'teet feey* the little girls

Note.—1. Nouns and adjectives in the plural take the ending "s." This "s" is mute.

2. Before any plural noun, whether masculine or feminine, the word for "the" in French is *les*.

3. *le* and *la* are replaced by *l'* before a vowel.

It and They

le crayon ; il est bleu	*le krai-yoN ; bl(ay)*	*ee-lai*	the pencil ; it is blue
la plume ; elle est jaune	*lah pl(ee)m ; zhohn*	*ai-lai*	the pen ; it is yellow

| les mouchoirs ; **ils** sont blancs | *lay moosh-wahr ; eel soN blaN* | the handkerchiefs ; they are white |
| les nappes ; elles sont blanches | *lay nahp ; ail soN blaNsh* | the tablecloths ; they are white |

Masculine		*Feminine*		
Sing.	*Plur.*	*Sing.*	*Plur.*	
le	les	la	les	the
il	ils	elle	elles	it, they

Special care must be taken with the translation of " it " and " they."

Use : *il* when " it " stands for a masculine noun in singular.
      elle when " it " stands for a feminine noun in singular.
      ils when " they " stands for masculine nouns in plural.
      elles when " they " stands for feminine nouns in plural.

For example, when translating " it is green" (" it " referring to the book, which is *le livre*, i.e. masculine in French), the word *il* is used for the translation of " it " : *il est vert*. But when " it " stands for the door, which is *la porte*, i.e. feminine, *elle* is used for the translation of " it," as in : *elle est verte*.

A, An

Masculine

un jardin	*(ai)N zhahr-daiN*	a garden
un journal	*(ai)N zhoor-nahl*	a newspaper
un cigare	*(ai)N see-gahr*	a cigar

Feminine

une maison	*(ee)n mai-zoN*	a house
une chaise	*(ee)n shaiz*	a chair
une cigarette	*(ee)n see-gah-rait*	a cigarette

Plural

des Français	*day fraN-sai*	Frenchmen ; French people
des allumettes	*day-zah-l(ee)mait*	matches
des journaux	*day zhoor-noh*	newspapers

Note.—1. *Un*, " a," " an," is used before a masculine noun.

2. *Une*, " a," " an," is used before a feminine noun.

3. In plural, where there is no article at all in English (books, horses, Englishmen), the French use a special form, *des*, which also means " some " or " any."

4. Words ending in " al " have their plural in " aux " (pronounced *oh*).

To be and Not to be

être *aitr* to be	**ne pas être** *ne pah-zaitr* not to be	

je suis content	*zhe swee koN-taN*	I am glad
vous êtes fatigué	*voo-zait fah-tee-gay*	You are tired
il est malade	*ee-lai mah-lahd*	He is ill
elle est belle	*ai-lai bail*	She is beautiful
nous sommes prêts	*noo som prai*	We are ready
ils sont Anglais	*eel soN-taN-glai*	They (masc.) are English
elles sont Anglaises	*ail soN-taN-glaiz*	They (fem.) are English

suis-je en retard ?	*swee zhe aN re-tahr*	Am I late ?
êtes-vous là ?	*ait voo lah*	Are you there ?
est-il Écossais ?	*ai-teel ay-ko-sai*	Is he a Scot ?
est-elle Française ?	*ai-tail fraN-saiz*	Is she French ?
sommes-nous tous ici ?	*som noo toos ee-see*	Are we all here ?
sont-ils Belges ?	*soN-teel bailzh*	Are they (masc.) Belgians ?
sont-elles Suisses ?	*soN-tail swees*	Are they (fem.) Swiss ?

Order of Words

A foreign language is not a word-for-word rendering of your own. Most things are expressed differently and the order of words in a sentence is not always the same. Sometimes more words are required to express the same idea, sometimes fewer.

Do you speak ? is **Parlez-vous ?** (= Speak you?) (*pahr-lay voo*).

I am not speaking is **Je ne parle pas** (*zhe ne pahrl pah*).

He is sleeping is **Il dort** (*eel dor*).

Note from the above examples that :

1. The verb " to do " is not used in French to form questions or to make negative statements.

2. No difference is made between " she does not speak " and " she is not speaking " : *elle ne parle pas* translates both.

PART I

FRENCH—ENGLISH

GREETINGS AND LEAVE-TAKING

THE French are extremely polite. It is considered rude to answer merely **oui** or **non**. Every **oui** or **non** is followed by either **monsieur** (when talking to a man), or **madame** (to a married woman), or **mademoiselle** (to an unmarried woman).

The same applies to greetings. " Good day " (or " Good morning," or " Good afternoon ") is **Bonjour** (*boN-zhoor*), **monsieur** (*miss-y(ay)*), or **madame** (*mah-dahm*), or **mademoiselle** (*mahd-mwah-zail*).

" Good evening " is **Bonsoir** (*boN-swahr*) **monsieur** (**madame, mademoiselle**).

" Good night " is **Bonne nuit** (*bon nwee*) **monsieur** (**madame, mademoiselle**).

" Goodbye " or " Cheerio " is **Au revoir** (*oh re-vwahr*) **monsieur** (**madame, mademoiselle**).

A demain	*ah d'maiN*	Till to-morrow
A ce soir	*ah se swahr*	Till this evening
A bientôt	*ah byaiN-toh*	Till soon (i.e. see you soon ; so long)

THANKS AND APOLOGIES

Merci	*mair-see*	Thanks
Merci beaucoup	*mair-see boh-koo*	Thanks very much
Vous êtes bien aimable	*voo-zait byai-nai-mahbl*	You are very kind
Je vous remercie	*zh'voo re-mair-see*	I thank you
Il n'y a pas de quoi	*eel nyah pah de kwah*	Don't mention it (lit. "There is not of what ")

Note.—If you are offered anything and wish to accept : **avec plaisir** (*ah-vaik plai-zeer*) with pleasure ; **vous êtes bien aimable** (see above). If you refuse, say : **merci** or **merci bien.**

Pardon	*pahr-doN*	Sorry
Excusez-moi	*aiks-k(ee)-zay mwah*	Excuse me
Je vous demande pardon	*zh'voo d'maNd pahr-doN*	I beg your pardon ; I apologize
Je regrette beaucoup	*zhe re-grait boh-koo*	I am very sorry
Pardonnez-moi	*pahr-do-nay mwah*	Forgive me

Note.—For " I beg your pardon " in the sense of " Please repeat what you said ; I did not understand you very well," say : **Plaît-il ?** (*plai-teel*) or **Vous dites ?** (*voo deet*).

APPROVAL AND DISAPPROVAL

Oui	*wee*	Yes
Non	*noN*	No
Bon	*boN*	Good ! All right !
Très bien	*trai byaiN*	Very well
C'est ça	*sai sah*	That's it. That's right
C'est vrai	*sai vrai*	That's true
C'est beau	*sai boh*	It's beautiful
C'est joli	*sai zho-lee*	It's pretty
C'est charmant	*sai shahr-maN*	It's charming
C'est merveilleux	*sai mair-vai-y(ay)*	It's wonderful
C'est excellent	*sai-taik-se-laN*	It's excellent
C'est délicieux	*sai day-lees-y(ay)*	It's delicious
C'est drôle	*sai drohl*	It's funny
Ce n'est pas mal	*s'nai pah mahl*	It is not bad
Ce n'est pas bon	*s'nai pah boN*	It is not good
Ce n'est pas vrai	*s'nai pah vrai*	It is not true
Je sais	*zhe sai*	I know
Je ne sais pas	*zhen'sai pah*	I don't know
Je comprends	*zhe koN-praN*	I understand
Je ne comprends pas	*zhen'koN-praN pah*	I don't understand
Je ne vous comprends pas	*zhe ne voo koN-praN pah*	I don't understand you
Je l'aime	*zhe laim*	I like it
Je ne l'aime pas	*zhe ne laim pah*	I don't like it
Certainement	*sair-tain-maN*	Certainly
Certainement pas	*sair-tain maN pah*	Certainly not
Naturellement	*nah-t(ee)-rail'maN*	Naturally. Of course
Naturellement pas	*nah-t(ee)-rail'maN pah*	Of course not !
Peut-être	*p(ay)-taitr*	Perhaps. Maybe
Pas du tout	*pah d(ee) too*	Not at all
Si vous voulez	*see voo voo-lay*	If you like
Comme vous voulez	*kom voo voo-lay*	As you like
Ça m'est égal	*sah mai-tai-gahl*	It's all the same to me. Just as you like
Je le crois	*zhe le krwah*	I believe so
Je le suppose	*zhe le s(ee)-pohz*	I suppose so
Je l'espère	*zhe lais-pair*	I hope so
Ça dépend	*sah day-paN*	It depends
D'accord !	*dah-kor*	Agreed. All right. O.K.

Il est gentil	ee-lai zhaN-tee	He is nice
Ils sont gentils	eel soN zhaN-tee	They are nice (m.)
Elle est gentille	ai-lai zhaN-teey	She is nice
Elles sont gentilles	ail soN zhaN-teey	They are nice (f.)
C'est mauvais	sai moh-vai	It is bad
sale	sahl	dirty
horrible	o-reebl	horrible
dégoûtant	day-goo-taN	disgusting
laid	lai	ugly
désagréable	day-zah-gray-ahbl	unpleasant
Vous n'êtes pas du tout aimable	voo nait pah d(ee) too ai-mahbl	You are not at all kind

QUESTIONS AND ANSWERS

Venez-vous ?	*ve-nay voo*	Are you coming ?
Mangez-vous ?	*maN-zhay voo*	Are you eating ?
Restez-vous ?	*rais-tay voo*	Are you staying ?
Dormez-vous ?	*dor-may voo*	Are you sleeping ?
Jouez-vous ?	*zhoo-ay voo*	Are you playing ?
Vous venez (n'est-ce pas ?)	*voo v'nay (nais pah)*	You are coming, aren't you ?
mangez	*maN-zhay*	eating
restez	*rais-tay*	staying
dormez	*dor-may*	sleeping
jouez	*zhoo-ay*	playing
Oui, je viens	*(w)ee zhe vyiN*	Yes, I am coming
mange	*maNzh*	eating
reste	*raist*	staying
dors	*dor*	sleeping
joue	*zhoo*	playing
Non, je ne viens pas	*noN zh'ne vyiN pah*	No, I am not coming
mange	*maNzh*	eating
reste	*raist*	staying
dors	*dor*	sleeping
joue	*zhoo*	playing

Ne...pas = not.   Ne precedes the verb and **pas** follows it.

Êtes-vous Français(e) ?	*ait voo fraN-sai(z)*	Are you French ?
occupé(e) ?	*oh-k(ee)pay*	busy ?
libre ?	*leebr*	free ?
prêt(e) ?	*prai(t)*	ready ?
fatigué(e) ?	*fah-tee-gay*	tired ?
malade ?	*mah-lahd*	ill ?
Vous êtes Français(e), n'est-ce pas ?	*voo-zait fraN-sai(z) nais pah*	You are French, aren't you?
occupé(e) ?	*oh-k(ee)pay*	busy ?
libre ?	*leebr*	free ?
prêt(e) ?	*prai(t)*	ready ?
fatigué(e) ?	*fah-tee-gay*	tired ?
malade ?	*mahlahd*	ill ?

The letters in parentheses are added when speaking of women.

Je suis Français(e)	*zhe s(w)ee fraN-sai(z)*	I am French
occupé(e)	*oh-k(ee)pay*	busy
libre	*leebr*	free
etc.		etc.
Non, je ne viens pas	*noN zhe ne vyiN pah*	No, I am not coming
reste	*raist*	staying
dors	*dor*	sleeping
joue	*zhoo*	playing

QUESTIONS WITH "WHERE," "WHO," "WHAT," "WHICH," "WHY," ETC.

(1) WHERE ? Où ? *oo*

Où est-il ?	*oo ai-teel*	Where is he ?
Mon ami, où est-il ?	*mo-nah-mee oo ai-teel*	Where is my friend ?
Mes amis, où sont-ils ?	*may-zah-mee oo soN-teel*	Where are my friends ?
Où est-elle ?	*oo ai-tail*	Where is she ?
Madame Albert, où est-elle ?	*mah-dahm ahl-bair oo ai-tail*	Where is Mrs. Albert ?
Mademoiselle, où est-elle ?	*mahdmwah-zail oo ai-tail*	Where is the young lady ?
Les jeunes filles, où sont-elles ?	*lay zh(ai)n feey oo soN-tail*	Where are the girls ?
Les lampes, où sont-elles ?	*lay laNp oo soN-tail*	Where are the lamps ?
Où êtes-vous ?	*oo ait voo*	Where are you ?
Où sommes-nous ?	*oo som noo*	Where are we ?
Où allez-vous ?	*oo ah-lay voo*	Where are you going ?
D'où venez-vous ?	*doo v'nay voo*	Where do you come from ?
Où est la gare ?	*oo ai lah gahr*	Where is the station ?
la mairie ?	*lah mai-ree*	the town hall ?
le bureau de poste	*le b(ee)roh de post*	the post office ?

(2) WHO ? Qui ? *kee*, or Qui est-ce qui ? *kee ais kee*

Qui est le patron ?	*kee ai le paht-roN*	Who is the master of the place (the boss) ?
Qui est-ce ?	*kee ais*	Who is it ?
Qui est là ?	*kee ai lah*	Who is there ?
Qui est cet homme ?	*kee ai sai-tom*	Who is that man ?
Qui est cette femme ?	*kee ai sait fahm*	Who is that woman ?
Qui sont ces hommes ?	*kee soN sai-zom*	Who are these men ?
Qui sont ces femmes ?	*kee soN sai fahm*	Who are these women ?
Qui voyez-vous ?	*kee vwah-yay voo*	Whom do you see ?
Qui sait ça ?	*kee sai sah*	Who knows that ?
Qui dit ça ?	*kee dee sah*	Who says that ?

25

De qui parlez-vous ?	de kee pahr-lay voo	Of whom are you speaking ?
A qui parlez-vous ?	ah kee pahr-lay voo	To whom are you speaking ?
A qui est-ce ?	ah kee ais	To whom does this belong ?
Pour qui est-ce ?	poor kee ais	For whom is it ?
Avec qui vont-ils (elles) ?	ah-vaik kee voN-teel (-tail)	With whom do they go ?

(3) WHAT ? Que ? *ke*, or Qu'est-ce que ? *kais-ke*

Qu'est-ce que c'est ?	kaisk'sai	What is it ?
Qu'est-ce que	kaisk'	What
vous dites ?	voo deet	do you say ?
vous faites ?	voo fait	are you doing ?
vous mangez ?	voo maN-zhay	are you eating ?
vous buvez ?	voo b(ee)vay	are you drinking ?
vous jouez ?	voo zhoo-ay	are you playing ?
vous voulez ?	voo voo-lay	do you want ?
vous avez ?	voo-zah-vay	have you ?
il dit ?	eel dee	does he say ?
elle fait ?	ail fai	is she doing ?
ils mangent ?	eel maNzh	are they eating ?
elles boivent ?	ail bwahv	are they (f.) drinking ?
il y a ?	eel yah	is the matter ?

Alternative forms with **que** are : **Que dites-vous ? Que faites-vous ? Que mangez-vous ? Que buvez-vous ? Que jouez-vous ? Que dit-il ?** etc.

Note.—" What " in the combinations " with what," " of what," " to what," etc., is **quoi** *kwah* :

Avec quoi ?	ah-vaik kwah	With what ?
Devant quoi ?	de-vaN kwah	In front of what ?
Derrière quoi ?	dair-yair kwah	Behind what ?
De quoi ?	de kwah	Of what ? From what ?
A quoi ?	ah kwah	To what ?

(4) WHICH ? WHAT ? WHAT A . . . ! Quel [1] Quelle [2] Quels [3] Quelles [4]

kail (these four forms are pronounced alike)

| Quel jour sommes-nous ? | kail zhoor som noo | What day are we ? (What's to-day ?) |
| Quelle heure est-il ? | kai-l(ai)r ai-teel | What time is it ? |

[1] With a masculine noun (singular).   [3] With masculine nouns (plural).
[2] With a feminine noun (singular).   [4] With feminine nouns (plural).

A quelle heure	ah kai-l(ai)r	At what time
partez-vous ?	pahr-tay voo	are you leaving ?
vient-il ?	vyiN-teel	is he coming ?
viennent-ils ?	vyain-teel	are they coming ?
Quel est votre nom ?	kai-lai votr noN	What is your name ?
Quel est le nom de	kai-lai le noN de	What is the name of
cette ville ?	sait veel	this town ?
ce village ?	se vee-lahzh	this village ?
cet endroit ?	sai-taN-drwah	this place ?
Quel vilain temps !	kail vee-liN taN	What nasty weather !
Quel beau temps !	kail boh taN	What a beautiful day !
Quelle belle église !	kail bai-lay-gleez	What a beautiful church !
Quels beaux enfants !	kail boh-zaN-faN	What beautiful children !
Quelles belles fleurs !	kail bail fl(ai)r	What beautiful flowers !

Note.—There is no difference in French between " what a ... ! "
" which ... " and " what ... " when used as an adjective, i.e. in
connection with nouns. As with all adjectives, there is a special
form for the feminine, and in plural an *s* is added.

(5) HOW MUCH ? HOW MANY ? Combien ? *koN-byaiN*

Combien de kilo-mètres ?	koN-byaiN de kee-loh-maitr	How many kilometres ?
Combien d'argent ?	koN-byaiN dahr-zhaN	How much money ?
Combien d'hommes	koN-byaiN dom	How many men ?
Combien en avez vous ?	koN-byai-nah-nah-vay voo	How much (or many) have you got ?
Combien en voulez-vous ?	koN-byai-naN voo-lay voo	How much (or many) do you want ?
Combien de temps ?	koN-byaiN de taN	How much time ? (How long ?)
Combien est-ce ?	koN-byaiN ai-se	How much is it ?

(6) WHEN ? Quand ? *kaN*

Quand vient-il ?	kaN vyaiN-teel	When is he coming ?
Quand venez-vous ?	kaN ve-nay voo	When are you coming ?
Quand viennent-ils ?	kaN vyain-teel	When are they coming ?
Quand partez-vous ?	kaN pahr-tay voo	When are you leaving ?
Quand revenez-vous ?	kaN rev' nay voo	When are you coming back ?
Quand revient-il ?	kaN rev-yaiN-teel	When is he coming back ?
Quand reviennent-ils ?	kaN rev-yain-teel	When are they coming back ?

(7) WHY ?   Pourquoi ? *poor-kwah*

Pourquoi faites-vous ça ?	*poor-kwah fait voo sah*	Why do you do that ?
Pourquoi dites-vous ça ?	*poor-kwah deet voo sah*	Why do you say that ?
Pourquoi partez-vous déjà ?	*poor-kwah pahr-tay voo day-zhah*	Why are you leaving already ?
Pourquoi ça ?	*poor-kwah sah*	What is the reason of that ?
Pourquoi pas ?	*poor-kwah pah*	Why not ?

(8) HOW ?   Comment ? *ko-maN*

Comment ça va ?	*ko-maN sah vah*	How is it going ? (How are you ?)
Comment va	*ko-maN vah*	How is
monsieur votre père ?	*miss-y(ay) votr pair*	your father ?
madame votre mère ?	*mah-dahm votr mair*	your mother ?
Mademoiselle ?	*mahd-mwah-zail*	the young lady ?
votre fils ?	*votr fees*	your son ?
Comment vont	*ko-maN voN*	How are
les petits ?	*lay p'tee*	the little ones ?
vos frères ?	*voh frair*	your brothers ?
vos sœurs ?	*voh s(ai)r*	your sisters ?
Comment dites-vous ?	*ko-maN deet voo*	What's that you are saying ? What did you say ?
Comment ça ?	*ko-maN sah*	How's that ? How do you mean ?

(9) MISCELLANEOUS QUESTIONS

Est-ce que *aisk'* (is it that), when placed before a statement turns it into a question, e.g. :

Elle est Française	*ai-lai fraN saiz*	She is French.
Est-ce qu'elle est Française	*ais hai-lai fraN-saiz*	Is she French ?
[1] Est-ce que vous venez ?	*aisk' voo ve-nay*	Are you coming ?
[1] Est-ce que vous parlez français ?	*aisk' voo pahr-lay fraN-sai*	Do you speak French ?

[1] Alternative forms to these questions are : **Venez-vous ? Parlez-vous français ?**

[1]Est-ce que vous   *aish' voo koN-pre-nay*   Do you understand ?
  comprenez ?
[1]Est-ce que vous   *aish' voo poo-vay fair*   Can you do that ?
  pouvez faire ça ?   *sah*
[1]Est-ce que vous   *aish' voo poo-vay ray-*   Can you repair that ?
  pouvez réparer ça ?   *pah-ray sah*
Est-ce que vous   *aish' voo poo-vay me*   Can you give me that ?
  pouvez me don-   *do-nay sah*
  ner ça ?
Est-ce que vous   *aish' voo poo-vay me*   Can you lend me that ?
  pouvez me prê-   *prai-tay sah*
  ter ça ?
Est-ce que vous avez   *aish' voo-zah-vay*   Have you any
  du pain ?   *d(ee) piN*   bread ?
  de l'eau ?   *de loh*   water ?
  des cigarettes ?   *day see-gah-rait*   cigarettes ?
Est-ce que c'est bon ? *aish' sai boN*   Is it good ?
Est-ce qu'elle est   *ais-kail ai zhaN-teey*   Is she nice ?
  gentille ?
Est-ce que Monsieur   *aish' miss-y(ay) vil-*   Does   Mr.Williams   live
  Williams demeure   *yahms d'm(ai)r ee-*   here ?
  ici ?   *see*

[1] Alternative forms to these questions are : **Comprenez-vous ?**
Pouvez-vous faire ça ? Pouvez-vous réparer ça ? etc.

COMMANDS AND REQUESTS

You may add **s'il vous plaît** *seel voo plai* (if you please) to
each of the following :

Entrez	*aN-tray*	Come in. Go in
Sortez	*sor-tay*	Get out. Come out. Go out
Allez	*ah-lay*	Go. Go on. Get on with the job
Venez	*ve-nay*	Come
Venez ici	*ve-nay-zee-see*	Come here
Venez vite	*ve-nay veet*	Come quickly
Passez par là	*pah-say pahr lah*	Go through that way
Entrez par ici	*aN-tray pahr ee-see*	Come in this way
Restez	*rais-tay*	Stay where you are
Restez ici	*rais-tay-zee-see*	Stay here
Regardez	*re-gahr-day*	Look
Regardez ça	*re-gahr-day sah*	Look at that
Regardez-moi	*re-gahr-day mwah*	Look at me
Donnez-moi ça	*do-nay mwah sah*	Give me that
Parlez anglais	*pahr-lay-zaN-glais*	Speak English
Parlez plus haut	*pahr-lay pl(ee) oh*	Speak louder
Parlez plus lentement	*pahr-lay pl(ee) laNt-maN*	Speak more slowly
Prenez	*pre-nay*	Take that
Prenez-en deux	*pre-nay-zaN d(ay)*	Take two of them
Prenez-en davantage	*pre-nay-zaN dah-vaN-tahzh*	Take more of it (them)
Montrez-moi ça	*moN-tray mwah sah*	Show me that
Écoutez-moi	*ay-koo-tay mwah*	Listen to me
Attendez un moment	*ah-taN-day-zuN momaN*	Wait a moment
Attendez ici	*ah-taN-day-zee-see*	Wait here
Dites-le	*deet le*	Say it
Faites-le	*fait le*	Do it
Attention !	*ah-taN-syoN*	Look out ! Mind what you are doing !
Vite! Vite!	*veet veet*	Hurry ! Hurry !
Plus vite!	*pl(ee) veet*	Faster !
Encore plus vite!	*aN-kor pl(ee) veet*	Faster still !
Asseyez-vous	*ah-say-yay-voo*	Sit down
Levez-vous	*le-vay voo*	Get up. Stand up

HOW TO TRANSLATE

" Don't "

N'entrez pas !	*naN-tray pah*	Don't go in! Don't come in!
Ne sortez pas !	*ne sor-tay pah*	Don't go out! Don't come out!
N'allez pas !	*nah-lay pah*	Don't go!
Ne venez pas !	*ne ve-nay pah*	Don't come!
Ne regardez pas !	*ne re-gahr-day pah*	Don't look!
Ne le lui donnez pas !	*ne le lwee do-nay pah*	Don't give it to him!
Ne parlez pas si vite !	*ne pahr-lay pah see veet*	Don't speak so fast!
Pas si vite !	*pah see veet*	Not so fast !
Pas trop vite !	*pah troh veet*	Not too fast !
N'attendez pas !	*nah-taN-day pah*	Don't wait !
Ne faites pas ça !	*ne fait pah sah*	Don't do that !
Ne faites rien !	*ne fait ryiN*	Don't do anything !
Ne lui dites rien !	*ne lwee deet ryiN*	Don't tell him (her) anything !
Ne leur dites rien !	*ne l(air)r deet ryiN*	Don't tell them anything !
Ne partez pas !	*ne pahr-tay pah*	Don't go away !
Ne touchez pas !	*ne too-shay pah*	Don't touch !
Assez !	*ah-say*	Enough !
Pas assez !	*pah-zah-say*	Not enough !

Note.—1. The negative is expressed by two words, **ne** (**n'** before a vowel) and **pas**. Ne is placed before the verb and **pas** after it. If there is no verb, **pas** alone is used : **pas assez** = not enough.

2. To say " not anything " (or " nothing "), **ne** is placed before the verb and **rien** after it. If there is no verb, **rien** alone is used : **rien de nouveau** = nothing new ; no news.

" To have " and " To go "

	avoir *ah-vwahr*	to have
j'ai	*zhay*	I have
nous avons	*noo-zah-voN*	we have
vous avez	*voo-zah-vay*	you have
il (elle) a	*eel (ail) ah*	he (she) has
ils (elles) ont	*eel (ail) zoN*	they have

31

J'ai ceci	*zhay se-see*	I have this. I've got this
Avez-vous ça ?	*ah-vay voo sah*	Have you got that ?
J'ai faim	*zhay fiN*	I am hungry
J'ai soif	*zhay swahf*	I am thirsty
J'ai chaud	*zhay shoh*	I am warm
J'ai froid	*zhay frwah*	I am cold
Vous avez raison	*voo-zah-vay rai-zoN*	You are right
Il a mal	*ee-lah mahl*	He is in pain
Avez-vous compris ?	*ah-vay voo koN-pree*	Have you understood ?
L'avez-vous vu ?	*lah-vay voo v(ee)*	Have you seen it (him, her) ?
L'avez-vous pris ?	*lah-vay voo pree*	Have you taken it ?

aller *ah-lay* to go

je vais	*zhe vai*	I go, am going
nous allons	*noo-zah-loN*	we go, are going
vous allez	*voo-zah-lay*	you go, are going
il (elle) va	*eel (ail) vah*	he (she) goes, is going
ils (elles) vont	*eel (ail) voN*	they go, are going
Je vais à la gare	*zhe vai-zah lah gahr*	I am going to the station
Nous allons au village	*noo-zah-loN-zoh vee-lahzh*	We are going to the village
Allez-vous le faire ?	*ah-lay voo le fair*	Are you going to do it ?
Il va venir	*eel vah v'neer*	He will come. He is coming
Ils vont vite	*eel voN veet*	They are going fast
Comment allez-vous ?	*ko-maN-tah-lay voo*	How are you ?
Je vais bien	*zhe vai byiN*	I am well
Comment va-t-il ?	*ko-maN vah-teel*	How is he ?
Il va bien	*eel vah byiN*	He is well
Comment ça va ?	*ko-maN sah vah*	How are things ? How goes it ?
Ça va bien	*sah vah byiN*	I'm all right. I feel fine

" There is," " There are "

Il y a une chambre au premier étage	*eel-yah(ee)nshaNb-roh prem-yay-ray-tahzh*	There is one room on the first floor
Il y a deux chambres au deuxième	*eel-yah d(ay) shaNb-roh d(ay)z-yaim*	There are two rooms on the second
Y a-t-il une chambre au premier ?	*yah-tee-l(ee)n shaNb-roh prem-yay*	Is there a room on the first floor ?
Y a-t-il des chambres au deuxième ?	*yah-teel day shaNb-roh d(ay)z-yaim*	Are there any rooms on the second ?

Note that **il y a** stands for both " there is " and " there are."

" Some," " Any "

Voici du pain	*vwah-see d(ee) piN*	Here is (some) bread
Y a-t-il de la viande ?	*yah-teel de lah vyaNd*	Is there any meat ?
Avez-vous des cigarettes ?	*ah-vay voo day see-gah-rait*	Have you any cigarettes ?
Y a-t-il du sucre dans le café ?	*yah-teel d(ee) s(ee)kr daN le kah-fay*	Is there (any) sugar in the coffee ?
Voilà du chocolat, de la bière et des cigarettes	*vwah-lah d(ee) shoh-koh-lah dlah byair ay day see-gah-rait*	There is (some) chocolate, (some) beer, and (some) cigarettes

Whereas in English the words in brackets can be omitted, they are required in French ; **du** before masculine nouns, **de la** before feminines, **des** before plurals, and **de l'** before nouns beginning with a vowel.

After a verb used in the negative, **de** alone is used : **Il y a du café** *eel-yah d(ee) kah-fay* There is (some) coffee ; but : **Il n'y a pas de café** *eel nyah pahd kah-fay* There is no coffee.

Nous avons des oranges *noo-zah-voN day-zoh-raNzh* We have (some) oranges ; but : **Il n'y a pas d'oranges** *eel nyah pah doh-raNzh* There are no oranges.

Note.—Use **voici** and **voilà** when pointing out persons or things ; **il y a** when just mentioning them or talking about them.

" Much," " Little "

Il boit beaucoup de bière	*eel bwah boh-kood-byair*	He drinks a lot of beer
J'ai peu d'argent	*zhay p(ay) dahr-zhaN*	I have little money. I have not much money
Nous fumons beaucoup de cigarettes	*noo f(ee)moN boh-kood see-gah-rait*	We smoke many cigarettes
Il a mangé peu de pain	*ee-lah maN-zhay p(ay)d piN*	He has not eaten much bread
Une bouteille de vin	*(ee)n boo-taiy de viN*	A bottle of wine
Une livre de beurre	*(ee)n leevr de b(ai)r*	A pound of butter
Une douzaine d'œufs	*(ee)n doo-zain d(ay)*	A dozen eggs
Combien d'argent avez-vous ?	*koN-byiN dahr-zhaN-tah-vay voo*	How much money have you got ?
Combien de cigarettes y a-t-il ?	*koN-byiNd see-gah-rait yah-teel*	How many cigarettes are there ?

Note that expressions of quantity are followed by **de**.

R.F.—3

" Nobody," " No one "

Personne	*pair-son*	Nobody
Je ne vois personne	*zhe ne vwah pair-son*	I don't see anybody
Il n'y a personne	*eel nyah pair-son*	There isn't anybody
Beaucoup de per-sonnes	*boh-koo de pair-son*	Lots of people
Une autre personne	*(ee)-nohtr pair-son*	Somebody else. Another person

Note.—1. When **personne** is used in a sentence, **ne** is placed in front of the verb.

2. **Une personne** is " a person."

" More," " No more "

Plus de dix francs	*pl(ee) de dee fraN*	More than ten francs
Encore du pain s.v.p.	*aN-kor d(ee) paiN seel voo plai*	More bread, please
Y en a-t-il encore ?	*yah-nah-teel aN-kor*	Is there any more ?
Encore un peu	*aN-ko-r(ai)N p(ay)*	A little more
Encore beaucoup	*aN-kor boh-koo*	Many (much) more
Encore une fois	*aN-ko-r(ee)n fwah*	Once more
Plus jamais	*pl(ee) zhah-mai*	Never more
Plus de potage, merci	*pl(ee) de po-tahzh mair-see*	No more soup, thank you
Je n'en ai plus	*zhe naN nai pl(ee)*	I have no more
Plus rien	*pl(ee) ryiN*	Nothing left at all
Il n'y en a plus	*eel nyah-nah pl(ee)*	There is (are) no more

Note.—**Ne** preceding the verb and **plus** following it means " no more."

" Ever," " Never "

Je ne fume presque jamais	*zhe ne f(ee)m praisk' zha-mai*	I hardly ever smoke
Si jamais vous re-venez ici	*see zhah-mai voo rev'-nay-zee-see*	If ever you come here again
Jamais plus	*zhah-mai pl(ee)*	Never again
Je ne l'ai jamais vu	*zhe ne lai zhah-mai v(ee)*	I have never seen it (him, her)
Il ne vient jamais	*eel ne vyaiN zhah-mai*	He never comes

Note.—To say " never," place **ne** before and **jamais** after the verb.

" Here," " There "

Venez ici	*ve-nay-zee-see*	Come here
Restez ici	*rais-tay-zee-see*	Stay here
C'est ici	*sai-tee-see*	It's here. This is the place

Ce n'est pas ici	s'nai pah-zee-see	It isn't here. This isn't the place
Il n'est pas ici	eel nai pah-zee-see	He isn't here
Par ici	pah-ree-see	This way
Le voici	le vwah-see	Here it (he) is
La voici	lah vwah-see	Here she is
Les voici	lay vwah-see	Here they are
Me voici	me vwah-see	Here I am
Ici ou là ?	ee-see oo lah	Here or there ?
Qui est là ?	kee ai lah	Who is there ?
Par là	pahr lah	That way
Le voilà	le vwah-lah	There it (he) is
La voilà	lah vwah-lah	There she is
Les voilà	lay vwah-lah	There they are

Note that **voici** can mean both " here is " and " here are,"
voilà both " there is " and " there are."

EXCLAMATIONS

See also " Expressions of Approval and Disapproval " on
page 21.

Quel beau chapeau!	kail boh shah-poh	What a beautiful hat !
Comme il est beau!	kom ee-lai boh	How beautiful it is !
Quels beaux arbres!	kail boh-zahrbr	What beautiful trees !
Comme ils sont beaux!	ko-meel soN boh	How beautiful they are !
Quelle belle fille!	kail bail feey	What a beautiful girl !
Comme elle est belle!	ko-mai-lai bail	How beautiful she is !
Quelles belles fleurs!	kail bail fl(ai)r	What beautiful flowers !
Comme elles sont belles!	ko-mail soN bail	How beautiful they are !
Quel beau temps!	kail boh taN	What a lovely day !
Comme il fait chaud!	ko-meel fai shoh	How warm it is !
Quel sale temps!	kail sahl taN	What a nasty day !
Comme il fait froid!	ko-meel fai frwah	How cold it is !
Attention!	ah-taNs-yoN	Mind ! Look out !
Tiens!	tyaiN	Hullo ! Really !
Vraiment ?	vrai-maN	Indeed ? Is that so ?
Un moment!	(ai)N moh-maN	One moment !
Dites-donc!	deet doNk	I say ! Listen !
Allons donc!	ah-loN doNk	Nonsense ! Not a bit of it !
Pensez donc!	paN-say doNk	Just think !
Mon Dieu!	mon dy(ay)	Good gracious !
Hé! Holà!	ay ; o-lah	Hallo ! I say ! (to call somebody's attention)

WANTS AND WISHES

Je veux partir	zhe v(ay) pahr-teer	I want to leave
le faire	le fair	do it
manger	maN-zhay	eat
boire	bwahr	drink
fumer	f(ee)-may	smoke
dormir	dor-meer	sleep

Veuillez...	v(ay)-yay	Will you please . . .
Ayez la bonté de...	ay-yay lah boN-tay de	Have the kindness to . . .
Je voudrais...	zhe vood-rai	I should like to . . .
Voulez-vous... ?	voo-lay voo	Do you want to . . . ?
Voudriez-vous... ?	vood-ryai voo	Would you like to . . . ?
Que voulez-vous ?	ke voo-lay voo	What do you want ?
Que veut-il ?	ke v(ay)-teel	What does he want ?
Il veut jouer	eel v(ay) zhoo-ay	He wants to play
Auriez-vous l'obli- geance de... ?	ohr-yay voo lob-lee- zhaNs de	Would you be so kind as to . . . ?

LIKES AND DISLIKES

See also " Expressions of Approval and Disapproval " on page 21.

Aimez-vous	ai-may voo	Do you like
Paris ?	pah-ree	Paris ?
la France ?	la fraNs	France ?
le vin rouge ?	le vaiN roozh	red wine ?
les poissons ?	lay pwah-soN	fish ?
le tennis ?	le tai-nees	tennis ?
les fraises ?	lay fraiz	strawberries ?
Je l'aime bien	zhe laim byaiN	I like it very much
Je les aime	zhe lay-zaim	I like them
Mieux que...	my(ay) ke	Better than . . .
Mais je préfère...	mai zhe pray-fair	But I prefer . . .
Et j'aime le mieux...	ay zhaim le my(ay)	And I like . . . best
Je n'aime pas...	zhe naim pah	I don't like . . .
Je le (les) déteste	zhe le (lay) day-taist	I hate it (them)

PERMISSION

Est-ce que je peux... ?	*aisk' zhe p(ay)*	Can I . . . ?
Vous pouvez	*voo poo-vay*	You can (may)
le prendre	*le praNdr*	take it
le faire	*le fair*	do it
venir	*ve-neer*	come
y aller	*ee ah-lay*	go there
Je ne peux pas...	*zhe ne p(ay) pah*	I cannot . . .
Pouvons nous... ?	*poo-voN noo*	Can we . . . ?
Permettez-moi de...	*pair-mai-tay mwah de*	Allow me to . . .
Est-il permis de... ?	*ai-teel pair-mee de*	Is it allowed to . . . ?
Laissez-moi...	*lai-say mwah*	Let me . . .
Je vous en prie	*zhe voo-zaN pree*	By all means

NECESSITY

Faut-il attendre ?	*foh-teel ah-taNdr*	Do I have to wait ?
payer ?	*pai-yay*	Do we have to pay ?
partir ?	*pahr-teer*	Does one have to leave ?
y aller ?	*ee ah-lay*	Does one have to go there ?
l'attendre ?	*lah-taNdr*	Does one have to wait for it (him, her) ?
Est-ce nécessaire ?	*ai-se nay-sai-sair*	Is it necessary ?
obligatoire ?	*ob-lee-gaht-wahr*	compulsory ?
facultatif ?	*fah-k(ee)l-tah-teef*	optional ?

INQUIRY AND INFORMATION

See also " Asking One's Way " on page 65 ; " Asking Questions " on pages 23 to 29.

Où puis-je avoir... ?	*oo pwee zhe ahv-wahr*	Where can I get . . . ?
Quand puis-je avoir... ?	*kaN pwee zhe ahv-wahr*	When can I get . . .?
Comment puis-je avoir... ?	*ko-maN pwee zhe ahv-wahr*	How can I get . . . ?
Savez-vous si... ?	*sah-vay voo see*	Do you know if . . . ?
Comment s'appelle	*ko-maN sah-pail*	What is this
cette rue ?	*sait r(ee)*	street called ?
cette gare ?	*sait gahr*	station called ?
ce village ?	*se vee-lahzh*	village called ?
Qu'y a-t-il ?	*kee ah-teel*	What has happened ?
Qu'est-ce qu'il y a ?	*kais'keel yah*	What is the matter ?
A quoi cela sert-il ?	*ah kwah s'lah sair-teel*	What is that for ? What is the use of that ?
Pouvez-vous me	*poo-vay voo me*	Can you
dire... ?	*deer*	tell me . . . ?
donner... ?	*do-nay*	give me . . . ?
recommander... ?	*re-ko-maN-day*	recommend me . . . ?
vendre... ?	*vaNdr*	sell me . . . ?
Je voudrais me renseigner sur...	*zhe voo-drai me raN-sain-yay s(ee)r*	I should like to inquire about . . .
Pourriez-vous me donner des renseignements sur... ?	*poor-yay voo me do-nay day raN-sainy-maN s(ee)r*	Could you give me information about . . . ?
Le bureau de renseignements	*le b(ee)-roh de raN-sainy'maN*	the inquiry-office

MEETING PEOPLE—POLITE EXPRESSIONS

Permettez-moi de vous présenter...	*pair-mai-tay mwah de voo pray-zaN-tay*	Allow me to introduce . . . to you
Veuillez me présenter à monsieur (madame) ?	*v(ai)-yay me pray-zaN-tay ah mis-y(ay) (mah-dahm)*	Would you kindly introduce me to the gentleman (lady) ?
Enchanté de faire votre connaissance	*aN-shaN-tay de fair votr ko-nai-saNs*	(I am) pleased to make your acquaintance
J'espère avoir le plaisir de vous revoir	*zhais-pair av-wahr le plai-zeer de voo re-vwahr*	I hope to meet you again
Venez me voir demain, je vous prie	*ve-nay me vwahr de-miN zhe voo pree*	Come to see me to-morrow, please
A quelle heure êtes-vous chez vous ?	*ah kai-l(ai)r ait voo shay voo*	When are you at home ?
Monsieur... est-il chez lui ?	*miss-y(ay) ai-teel shay lwee*	Is Mr. . . . at home ?
Je voudrais parler à...	*zhe voo-drai pahr-lay ah*	I wish to see . . .
...est sorti(e)	*ai sor-tee*	. . . has gone out
A quelle heure va-t-il rentrer ?	*ah kai-l(ai)r vah-teel raN-tray*	When will he be back ?
Je reviendrai	*zhe re-vyiN-dray*	I shall call again
Qui dois-je annoncer ?	*kee dwah-zhe ah-noN-say*	What name shall I say ?
Veuillez remettre ma carte ?	*v(ay)-yay re-maitr mah kahrt*	Will you please send in my card ?
Donnez-vous la peine d'entrer ?	*do-nay voo la pain daN-tray*	Will you come in, please ?
Veuillez attendre un instant ?	*v(ay)-yay ah-taNdr (ai)N-naiNs-taN*	Will you please wait a few moments ?
Je vous demande pardon de vous avoir fait attendre	*zhe voo d'maNd pahr-doN de voo-zahv-wahr fai-tah-taNdr*	I am sorry to have kept you waiting
Je viens un peu tard	*zhe vyaiN (ai)N p(ay) tahr*	I am rather late
Je ne vous dérange pas ?	*zhe ne voo day-raNzh pah*	I am not disturbing you ?
Pas du tout	*pah d(ee) too*	Not at all

39

Asseyez-vous, s'il vous plaît	*ah-say-yay voo seel voo plai*	Please be seated
Qu'y a-t-il pour votre service ?	*kyah-teel poor votr sair-vees*	What can I do for you ?
Je suis venu vous dire que...	*zhe swee ve-n(ee) voo deer que*	I have come to tell you that . . .
Vous êtes bien aimable	*voo-zait byai-nai-mahbl*	That is very kind of you
Puis je vous offrir... ?	*p(w)ee zhe voo-zof-reer*	May I offer you . . . ?
Il est temps de vous dire au revoir	*ee-lai taN de voo deer oh r'vwahr*	I must be off now
Mes compliments à...	*may koN-plee-maN tah*	Kind regards to . . .
Merci, M..., je n'y manquerai pas	*mair-see, m..., zhe nee maNk'ray pah*	Thank you, I won't forget
Comment allez-vous ?	*ko-maN-tah-lay voo*	
Comment ça va-t-il	*ko-maN sah vah-teel*	How are you ?
Merci, M..., très bien	*mair-see, m..., trai byaiN*	Very well, thank you
Pas mal ; et vous ?	*pah mahl ay voo*	Not bad ; and you ?
Assez bien. J'ai été souffrant, mais je vais mieux	*ah-say byaiN zhay ay-tay soof-raN mai zhe vai my(ay)*	Quite well. I have been ill, but I am better now
Comment va Monsieur votre père ?	*ko-maN vah mis-yay votr pair*	How is your father ?
Madame votre mère ?	*mah-dahm votr mair*	mother ?
Merci, M..., chez nous tout le monde va bien	*mair-see, m..., shay noo too le moNd vah byaiN*	Thank you, everybody at home is well
Je suis heureux de l'apprendre	*zhe swee-z(ay)-r(ay) de lahp-raNdr*	I am pleased to hear it
Mon frère est malade	*moN frair-ai mah-lahd*	My brother is ill
Je regrette de l'apprendre	*zhe re-grait de lahp-raNdr*	I am sorry to hear it

SPEAKING AND UNDERSTANDING

Parlez-vous anglais ?	*pahr-lay voo aN-glai*	Do you speak English ?
Un peu seulement	*(ai)N p(ay) s(ai)l'maN*	Only a little
Y a-t-il quelqu'un qui parle anglais ?	*yah-teel kail-k(ai)N kee pahrl aN-glai*	Is there anybody who speaks English ?
Comprenez-vous ?	*koN-pre-nay voo*	Do you understand ?
Je comprends si vous parlez lente-ment	*zhe koN-praN see voo pahr-lay laNt-maN*	I understand if you speak slowly
Je ne comprends pas	*zhen'koN-praN pah*	I don't understand
Ne parlez pas si vite	*ne pahr-lay pah see veet*	Don't speak so fast
Comment dit-on... en anglais ?	*ko-maN-dee-toN ah-naN-glai*	What is . . . in English ?
Que veut dire... ?	*ke v(ay) deer*	What does . . . mean ?
Veuillez répéter	*v(ai)-yay ray-pay-tay*	Please repeat
expliquer	*aiks-plee-kay*	explain
leur dire	*l(ai)r deer*	tell them
lui demander	*lwee d'maN-day*	ask him (her)

HOW TO TRANSLATE

" Me," " You," " Him," " Her "

Il m'attend	*eel mah-taN*	He is expecting (waiting for) me
Il ne m'attend pas	*eel ne mah-taN pah*	He is not expecting (waiting for) me
Je vous connais	*zhe voo ko-nai*	I know you
Je ne vous connais pas	*zhe ne voo ko-nai pah*	I don't know you
Connaissez-vous ce monsieur ?	*ko-nai-say voo se mis-yay*	Do you know this gentleman ?
Le connaissez-vous ?	*le ko-nai-say voo*	Do you know him ?
Je le connais	*zhe le ko-nai*	I know him
Je ne le connais pas	*zhe ne le ko-nai pah*	I don't know him
Connaissez-vous cette dame ?	*ko-nai-say voo sait dahm*	Do you know that lady ?
La connaissez-vous ?	*lah ko-nai-say voo*	Do you know her ?
Je la connais	*zhe lah ko-nai*	I know her
Je ne la connais pas	*zhe ne lah ko-nai pah*	I don't know her
Je vous aime	*zhe voo-zaim*	I love you
Je l'aime	*zhe laim*	I love him (her, it)
Elle m'aime	*ail maim*	She loves me
Il ne m'aime pas	*eel ne maim pah*	He does not love me
Je ne vous aime pas	*zhe ne voo-zaim pah*	I don't love you

Note that **me** (me), **vous** (you), **le** (him), **la** (her) precede the verb. **Me, le, la** are changed to **m', l', l'** before a vowel or *h* mute.

" It," " Them "

Voici votre verre	*vwah-see votr vair*	Here is your glass
Prenez-le !	*pre-nay le*	Take it
Voici votre tasse	*vwah-see votr tahs*	Here is your cup
Prenez-la !	*pre-nay lah*	Take it
Voilà les allumettes	*vwah-lah lay-zah-l(ee)-mait*	Here are the matches
Prenez-les !	*pre-nay lay*	Take them
Ceci est mon journal	*se-see ai moN zhoor-nahl*	This is my newspaper

Ne le prends pas	*ne le praN pah*	Don't take it
C'est ma plume	*sai mah pl(ee)m*	It is my pen
Ne la prends pas	*ne lah praN pah*	Don't take it
Ce sont mes gants	*se soN may gaN*	They are my gloves
Ne les prends pas	*ne lay praN pah*	Don't take them
Voilà le billet	*vwah-lah le bee-yai*	There is the ticket
Le voilà	*le vwah-lah*	There it is
Voici les journaux	*vwah-see lay zhoor-noh*	Here are the newspapers
Les voici	*lay vwah-see*	Here they are
Voici la serveuse	*vwah-see lah sair-v(ay)z*	Here is the waitress
La voici	*lah vwah-see*	Here she is
Voilà les enfants	*vwah-lah lay-zaN-faN*	There are the children
Les voilà	*lay vwah-lah*	There they are

The personal pronouns **le** (him, it), **la** (her, it), **les** (them), etc., follow the verb in the Imperative, if it is in the Affirmative.

If the Imperative is in the Negative, all personal pronouns are placed between **ne** and the verb.

" To him," " To her," " To them "

Dites-lui...	*deet lwee*	Tell him . . . ; Tell her . . .
Dites-leur...	*deet l(ai)r*	Tell them . . .
Écrivez-lui...	*ay-kree-vay lwee*	Write to him (her)
Parlez-leur...	*pahr-lay l(ai)r*	Speak to them
Demandez	*d'maN-day*	Ask
Répondez	*ray-poN-day*	Answer
Ne lui parlez pas	*ne lwee pahr-lay pah*	Don't speak to him (her)
Ne leur répondez pas	*ne l(ai)r ray poN-day pah*	Don't reply to them
Demandons-lui	*d'maN-doN lwee*	Let us ask him (her)
Leur écrivez-vous ?	*l(ai)r-ay-kree-vay voo*	Are you writing to them ?
Je ne leur écris pas	*zhe ne l(ai)-ray-kree pah*	I am not writing to them
Ils (elles) lui parlent	*eel (ail) lwee pahrl*	They are speaking to him (her)
Nous leur écrivons	*noo l(ai)-ray-kree-voN*	We are writing to them

In the same way as **me, le, la, les** the words **lui** (to him or to her) and **leur** (to them) precede the verb or the negative imperative.

" Of the," " To the "

La femme du pro-fesseur	*lah fam d(ee) pro-fai-s(ai)r*	The teacher's wife
La maison de mon père	*lah mai-zoN de moN pair*	My father's house
Le parapluie de la dame	*le pah-rah-plwee de lah dahm*	The lady's umbrella
Les parents des en-fants	*lay pah-raN day-zaN-fan*	The children's parents
Les souliers de l'en-fant	*lay sool-yay de laN-faN*	The child's shoes
Le nom de l'hôtel	*le noN de loh-tail*	The name of the hotel
Envoyez-le à cette adresse	*aN-vwah-yay le ah sai-tah-drais*	Send it to this address
Parlez au monsieur	*pahr-lay oh mis-y(ay)*	Speak to the gentleman
Demandez à la dame	*d'maN-day ah lah dahm*	Ask the lady
Répondez aux en-fants	*ray-poN-day oh-zaN-faN*	Answer the children
Retournons à l'hôtel	*re-toor-noN ah loh-tail*	Let us go back to the hotel

Note.—1. " The teacher's wife " must be turned into " the wife of the teacher," " My father's house " into " the house of my father," etc.

2. When **de** or **à** precede **le** or **les** the following contracted forms are used :

> **du** instead of **de le**
> **des** ,, ,, **de les**
> **au** ,, ,, **à le**
> **aux** ,, ,, **à les**

No contractions are used for **de là, de l', à la, à l'**.

3. Whereas in English the " to " is omitted in sentences like " He sends the lady flowers," it must not be left out in French. The same applies to the verbs **dire** (to tell), **demander** (to ask), **répondre** (to answer), and others. It is not difficult to under-stand why these require **à** (to) if we realize that they also mean " to speak to," " to put a question to," " to reply to."

" This," " That," " These," " Those "

Ce livre est très in- téressant	*se leev-rai trai-zaiN- tay-rai-saN*	This book is very interest- ing
Cette lettre est pour vous	*sait lait-rai poor voo*	This letter is for you
Ces enveloppes sont déchirées	*say-zaN-v'lop soN day-shee-ray*	These envelopes are torn
Ces chaises sont réservées	*say shaiz soN ray- zair-vay*	These chairs are reserved
Cet hôtel est trop cher	*sai-toh-tail ai troh shair*	This hotel is too expensive

Note from the above examples that **ce** is used with masculine nouns, **cette** with feminines, and **cet** with masculine nouns beginning with a vowel or mute *h*. The plural is **ces** in every case.

Ce livre can mean both " this book " and " that book," **cet enfant** both " this child " and " that child," **ces crayons** both " these pencils " and " those pencils." To emphasize the distinction between " this " and " that," " those " and " these "— -ci or -là are added to the noun. Compare the following :

Ce couteau-ci	*se koo-toh see*	This knife
Ce couteau-là	*se koo-toh lah*	That knife
Cette fourchette-ci	*sait foor-shait see*	This fork
Cette fourchette-là	*sait foor-shait lah*	That fork
Cet homme-ci	*sai-tom si*	This man
Cet homme-là	*sai-tom lah*	That man
Ces hommes-ci	*say nom see*	These men
Ces hommes-là	*say-zom lah*	Those men

If " this " and " that," " these " and " those " are used by themselves, i.e. not in connection with nouns, special forms are used as given in the following examples :

Ceci est pour moi	*se-see ai poor mwah*	This is for me
Cela est pour vous	*se-lah ai poor voo*	That is for you
Ceux-ci sont pour lui	*s(ay)-see soN poor lwee*	These (m.) are for him
Celles-ci sont pour elle	*sail see soN poor ail*	These (f.) are for her
Ceux-là sont pour nous	*s(ay)lah soN poor noo*	Those (m.) are for us
Celles-là sont pour nous	*sail lah soN poor noo*	Those (f.) are for us

" My," " Your," " His," " Her," etc.

Mon frère	*moN frair*	My brother
Ma sœur	*ma s(ai)r*	My sister
Mon oncle	*mo-noNkl*	My uncle
Mes parents	*may pah-raN*	My parents ; my relatives
Mon chapeau	*moN-shah-poh*	My hat
Ma canne	*mah kahn*	My walking stick
Mes gants	*may gaN*	My gloves
Son père	*soN pair*	His or her father
Sa mère	*sah mair*	His or her mother
Ses enfants	*say-zaN-faN*	His or her children
Son argent	*so-nahr-zhaN*	His or her money
Ses livres	*say leevr*	His or her books
Votre tante	*votr taNt*	Your aunt
Votre stylo	*votr stee-loh*	Your fountain-pen
Vos cigarettes	*voh-see-gah-rait*	Your cigarettes
Notre jardin	*notr zhahr-daiN*	Our garden
Nos enfants	*noh-zaN-faN*	Our children
Leur cousin	*l(ai)r koo-zaiN*	Their cousin
Leurs petits-enfants	*l(ai)r p'tee-zaN-faN*	Their grandchildren

The possessive adjectives (my, your, his, etc.), like any other adjectives in French, agree in gender with the thing possessed. **Son chapeau** is both " His hat " and " Her hat," because **chapeau** is masculine in French ; **sa tasse** stands for both " his " and " her cup," as **tasse** is feminine in French.

" Mine," " Yours," " His," " Hers," etc.

Ceci est à moi	*se-see ai-tah mwah*	This is mine
Cela est à vous	*se-lah ai-tah voo*	That is yours
Ceux-ci sont à lui	*s(ay)-see soN-tah l(w)ee*	These (m.) are his
Celles-ci sont à elle	*sail see soN-tah ail*	These (f.) are hers
Ceux-là sont à nous	*s(ay) lah soN-tah noo*	Those (m.) are ours
Celles-là sont à eux	*sail lah soN-tah (ay)*	Those (f.) are theirs (m.)
Ceci est à elles	*se-see ai-tah ail*	This is theirs (f.)

" Myself," " Yourself," " Himself," etc.

Je le ferai moi-même	*zhe le fe-ray mwah maim*	I shall do it myself
Le ferez-vous vous-même ?	*le fe-ray voo voo maim*	Will you do it yourself ?
Il le fera lui-même	*eel le fe-rah lwee maim*	He will do it himself

Elle le fera elle-même	*ail le fe-rah ail maim*	She will do it herself
Nous le ferons nous-mêmes	*noo le fe-roN noo maim*	We shall do it ourselves
Ils le font eux-mêmes	*eel le foN-t(ay) maim*	They are doing it themselves (m. and f.)
Elles le font elles-mêmes	*ail le foN-tail maim*	

" Isn't it ? " " Don't you ? " " Aren't you ? " " Isn't he ? " " Doesn't she ? " etc.

Vous êtes Français, n'est-ce pas ?	*voo-zait fraN-sai nais pah*	You are French, aren't you ?
Vous parlez anglais, n'est-ce pas ?	*voo pahr-lay-zaN-glai nais pah*	You speak English, don't you ?
C'est joli, n'est-ce pas ?	*sai zho-lee nais pah*	It is pretty, isn't it ?
Elle a reçu l'argent, n'est-ce pas ?	*ai-lah re-s(ee) lahr-zhaN nais pah*	She has received the money, hasn't she ?
Vous venez ce soir, n'est-ce pas ?	*voo v'nay se swahr nais pah*	You'll come this evening, won't you ?

Note.—N'est-ce pas ? is short for N'est-ce pas vrai ?=Is it not true ?

" It is . . .," " It was . . ."

1. C'est	bon	*sai*	*boN*	It is	good
C'était	bien	*say-tai byaiN*		It was	all right
	facile	*fah-seel*			easy
	difficile	*dee-fee-seel*			difficult
	vrai	*vrai*			true
	curieux	*k(ee)r-y(ay)*			strange
	drôle	*drohl*			funny
	amusant	*ah-m(ee)-zaN*			amusing
	mon professeur	*moN proh-fai-s(ai)r*			my teacher
Est-ce votre sac ?		*ai-se votr sahk*		Is it your handbag ?	
Était-ce votre chaise ?		*ay-tai se votr shaiz*		Was it your chair ?	

Note.—" It is " = C'est if followed by a noun, or by an adjective, provided the word " it " does not replace a noun (as in the following examples).

2. **Le verre—il est cassé**   *le vair ee-lai kah-say*   The glass—it is broken

    il était cassé   *ee-lay-tai kah-say*   it was broken

Note.—" It is " = **il est** when " it " replaces a masculine noun.

3. **La clé—elle est perdu**   *la klay ai-lai pair-d(ee)*   The key—it is lost

    elle était perdu   *ai-lay-tai pair-d(ee)*   it was lost

Note.—" It is " = **elle est** when " it " replaces a feminine noun.

4. **Il est six heures**   *ee-lai see-z(ai)r*   It is six o'clock

   Il était midi   *ee-lay-tai mee-dee*   It was noon

         tard   *tahr*   late

         presque minuit   *praish'meen-wee*   nearly midnight

Note.—" It is " = **il est** when speaking of time.

5. **Il fait beau**   *eel fait boh*   It is fine

   Il faisait mauvais   *eel fe-zai moh-vai*   It was nasty

        chaud   *shoh*   hot

        froid   *frwah*   cold

        du vent   *d(ee) vaN*   windy

Note.—" It is " = **il fait** when speaking of the weather.

6. **Il pleut**   *eel pl(ay)*   It is raining

   neige   *naizh*   snowing

   gèle   *zhail*   freezing

   dégèle   *day-zhail*   thawing

   Il pleuvait   *eel pl(ay)-vai*   It was raining

   neigeait   *nai-zhai*   snowing

   gelait   *zhe-lai*   freezing

   dégelait   *day-zhe-lai*   thawing

" Did you . . . ? " " I didn't . . . "

1. **Avez-vous commencé ?**   *ah-vay voo ko-maN-say*   Did you start ?

   Je n'ai pas fini   *zh'nay pah fee-nee*   I didn't finish

        mangé   *maN-zhay*   eat

        payé   *pai-yay*   pay

   L'avez vous pris   *lah-vay voo pree*   Did you take it ?

   Je ne l'ai pas fait   *zhe ne lay pah fai*   I didn't do it

        trouvé   *troo-vay*   find it

        acheté   *ahsh-tay*   buy it

        payé   *pai-yay*   pay for it

2. Êtes-vous allé ?	*ait vooz-ah-lay*	Did you go ?
Je ne suis pas venu	*zhen'swee pah ve-n(ee)*	I didn't come
sorti	*sor-tee*	go out
parti	*pahr-tee*	leave
Je suis allé chez le coiffeur	*zhe swee-zah-lay shay le kwah-f(ai)r*	I went to the hairdresser's
Je suis venu hier soir	*zhe swee ve-n(ee) yair swahr*	I came last night
Elle est sortie après le déjeuner	*ai-lai sor-tee ahp-rai le day-zh(ai)-nay*	She went out after lunch
Ils sont parti de bonne heure	*eel soN pahr-tee de bo-n(ai)r*	They left early
3 Vous êtes-vous coupé ?	*voo-zait voo koo-pay*	Did you cut yourself ?
Je ne me suis pas brûlé	*zhen me swee pah br(ee)-lay*	I didn't burn myself
Je ne me suis pas fait mal	*zhen me swee pah fai mahl*	I didn't hurt myself
Je ne me suis pas amusé	*zhen me swee pa zah-m(ee)-zay*	I didn't enjoy myself

Note.—1. **Avez-vous... ?** is the usual translation for " Did you ? " **Je n'ai pas...** for " I didn't."

2. **Êtes-vous... ? Je ne suis pas...** are used with verbs denoting movement from one place to another (to come, to go, to climb, to fall, etc.).

3. **Vous êtes-vous... ? Je ne me suis pas...** are used with reflexive verbs, i.e. verbs where the action is done by yourself and to yourself.

" I shall . . .," " Will you ? "

1. Je vais sortir	*zhe vai sor-teer*	I am going to	go out
jouer ?	*zhoo-ay*	(I shall)	play
Allez-vous l'acheter ?	*ah-lay voo lahsh-tay*	Are you going to	buy it ?
le faire ?	*le fair*	(Will you)	do it ?
le chercher ?	*le shair-shay*		fetch it ?
les voir ?	*lay vwahr*		see them ?
Il va vous en acheter	*eel vah voo-zaN-nahsh-tay*	He is going to	buy you some
Nous allons la chercher	*noo-zah-loN lah shair-shay*	We are going to look for her	
Ils vont partir	*eel voN pahr-teer*	They are going to leave	

R.F.—4

2. **Je partirai de-**   *zhe pahr-tee-ray de-*   I shall leave to-morrow
   main   *maiN*
   Irez-vous aussi ?   *ee-ray voo-zoh-see*   Will you go too ?
   Il viendra mardi   *eel vyaiN-drah mahr-*   He will come on Tuesday
                           dee
   Nous irons à pied   *noo-zee-roN-zah pyay*   We shall go on foot
   Ils ne viendront   *eel ne vyaiN-droN pah*   They will not come
   pas

Note.—1. The immediate future is expressed by **je vais**, " I am
going to."

2. The future tense of verbs is expressed by endings added to
the verb, and not as in English by special words (shall, will).

NUMBERS

0	zéro	*zay-roh*	11	onze	*oNz*
1	un	*(ai)N*	12	douze	*dooz*
2	deux	*d(ay)*	13	treize	*traiz*
3	trois	*trwah*	14	quatorze	*kah-torz*
4	quatre	*kahtr*	15	quinze	*kaiNz*
5	cinq	*saiNk*	16	seize	*saiz*
6	six	*sees*	17	dix-sept	*dee sait*
7	sept	*sait*	18	dix-huit	*dee-zweet*
8	huit	*weet*	19	dix-neuf	*deez n(ai)f*
9	neuf	*n(ai)f*	20	vingt	*vaiN*
10	dix	*dees*	21	vingt-et-un	*vaiN-tay uN*

22	vingt-deux	*vaiNt d(ay)*
23	vingt-trois	*vaiN trwah*
30	trente	*traNt*
31	trente-et-un	*traN-tay uN*
32	trente-deux	*traNt d(ay)*
40	quarante	*kah-raNt*
50	cinquante	*saiN-kaNt*
60	soixante	*swah-saNt*
70	soixante-dix	*swah-saNt dees*
71	soixante-onze	*swah-saNt oNz*
72	soixante-douze	*swah-saNt dooz*
73	soixante-treize	*swah-saNt traiz*
79	soixante-dix-neuf	*swah-saNt deez n(ai)f*
80	quatre-vingts	*kahtr vaiN*
90	quatre-vingt-dix	*kahtr vaiN dees*
91	quatre-vingt-onze	*kahtr vaiN oNz*
92	quatre-vingt-douze	*kahtr vaiN dooz*
100	cent	*saN*
200	deux cents	*d(ay) saN*
1,000	mille	*meel*
in 1948	en dix-neuf cent quarante-huit	*aN deez n(ai)f saN kah-raN weet*

1st	premier, première	*prem-yay prem-yair*
2nd	second, seconde or deuxième	*zgoN zgoNd d(ay)z-yaim*
3rd	troisième	*trwahz-yaim*
4th	quatrième	*kahtr-yaim*
5th	cinquième	*saiNk-yaim*

51

6th	sixième	*seez-yaim*
7th	septième	*sait-yaim*
8th	huitième	*weet-yaim*
9th	neuvième	*n(ai)v-yaim*
10th	dixième	*deez-yaim*

Note.—The first of a month is **le premier,** but the second, third, etc. **le deux, le trois,** etc. (see page 102).

WEIGHTS AND MEASURES

un kilogramme or kilo = 1,000 grammes = 2·2 lb.   *(ai)N kee-loh-grahm kee-loh meel grahm*

un demi-kilo or une livre = 500 grammes = 1·1 lb.   *(ai)N d'mee kee-loh (ee)n leevr*

un quintal métrique = 100 kilos = 2 cwt.   *(ai)N kiN-tahl mayt-reek*

1 ounce = 28 grammes ; 1 pound = 453 grammes ; 1 cwt. = 508 kilos

lourd	*loor*	heavy
léger	*lay-zhay*	light
peser	*pe-zay*	to weigh
le poids	*pwah*	the weight
une balance	*bah-laNs*	scales

1 mètre = 100 centimètres = 1,000 millimètres = 39 inches   *(ai)N maitr saN saN-tee-maitr meel mee-lee-maitr*

1 centimètre = 10 millimètres = $\frac{2}{5}$ inch (approx.)   *(ai)N saN-tee-maitr dee mee-lee-maitr*

1 kilomètre = 1,000 mètres = $\frac{5}{8}$ of a mile   *(ai)N kee-loh-maitr meel maitr*

1 inch = 2½ centimètres ; 1 foot = 30 centimètres (approx.)

1 yard = 90 centimètres (approx.) ; 5 miles = 8 kilomètres (approx.)

long (court)	*loN (koor)*	long (short)
large (étroit)	*lahrzh (ay-trwah)*	wide (narrow)
haut (profond)	*oh (pro-foN)*	high (deep)
cinq mètres de long sur trois mètres de large	*siN maitr de loN s(ee)r trwah maitr de lahrzh*	5 metres long by 3 metres wide

1 litre	*leetr* = 1¾ pints	1 pint	= (approx.) ⅛ litre
2 litres	= 3½ pints	1 quart	= ,, 1 litre
5 litres	= 1 gallon ¾ pints	1 gallon	= ,, 4½ litres

NOTICES

Entrée	Entrance
Sortie	Exit
Ouvert	Open
Fermé	Shut
Fumeurs	Smokers
Non-fumeurs	Non-smokers
Poussez	Push
Tirez	Pull
Défense de fumer	Smoking prohibited
Défense de cracher	Do not spit
Défense d'afficher	Billposting prohibited
Cabinet	Lavatory
Occupé	Engaged
Libre	Free
Chaud	Hot
Froid	Cold
Entrée interdite au public	No admittance
A vendre	For sale
A louer	To let
Entrez sans frapper	Walk in without knocking
Tournez le bouton s.v.p.	Please turn the handle
Essuyez vos pieds, s.v.p.	Please wipe your feet
Arrêt fixe	Bus (or tram) stop
Arrêt facultative	Stop by request
Prenez garde à la peinture	Wet paint
Tenir les chiens en laisse	Dogs must be led
Sens interdit	No entry
Sens unique	One-way street
Rue barrée	No thoroughfare

FOOD AND DRINK

The following list is arranged alphabetically to enable a better understanding of French menus. If the name of a dish is not found under the first word, it should be looked up under the second, e.g. " suprême de poulet " under " poulet."

abattis (m.pl.)	*ah-bah-tee*	giblets
ablette (f.)	*ah-blait*	bleak
abricots (m.pl.)	*ah-bree-koh*	apricots
agneau (m.)	*ahn-yoh*	lamb
aiglefin (m.)	*aigl-faiN*	haddock
ail (m.)	*ahy*	garlic
aile (f.)	*ail*	wing of poultry
aloyau (m.)	*al-wah-yoh*	sirloin (of beef)
amande (f.)	*ah-maNd*	almond
anchois (m.)	*aN-shwah*	anchovy
andouille (f.)	*aN-dooy*	chitterlings made into sausages
anguille (f.)	*aN-geey*	eel
ananas (m.)	*ah-nah-nah*	pineapple
artichauds (m.pl.)	*ahr-tee-shoh*	artichokes
asperge (f.)	*ahs-pairzh*	asparagus
assiette assortie	*ahs-yai-tah-sor-tee*	assortment of cold tongue, ham and beef
aubergine (f.)	*oh-bair-zheen*	fruit of the egg plant
baba (m.)	*bah-bah*	kind of sponge cake steeped in rum syrup
banane (f.)	*bah-nahn*	banana
barbue (f.)	*bahr-(bee)*	brill
bécasse (f.)	*bay-kahs*	woodcock
bécassine (f.)	*bay-kah-seen*	snipe
beignets (m.pl.)	*bain-yay*	fritters
betterave (f.)	*bait'rahv*	beetroot
beurre (m.)	*b(ai)r*	butter
au beurre	*oh b(ai)r*	cooked in butter
au beurre noir	*oh (b(ai)r nwahr*	with browned butter sauce
bifteck (m.)	*beef-taik*	beefsteak
aux pommes	*oh pom*	steak and chips

bisque	*beesk*	shell-fish soup
blanc-manger (m.)	*blaN-maN-zhay*	blancmange
blanquette (f.)	*blaN-kait*	stew of veal with sauce
bœuf (m.)	*b(ai)f*	beef
à la mode	*ah lah mod*	stewed beef
bombe glacée	*boNb glah-say*	ice pudding
bouchée (f.)	*boo-shay*	pie or patty
à la reine	*ah lah rain*	poultry pie
boudin (m.)	*boo-daiN*	black pudding
bouillabaise (f.)	*boo-yah-bais*	soup or stew of fish with tomatoes, onions and garlic
bouilli (m.)	*boo-yee*	boiled beef
bouillie (f.)	*boo-yee*	gruel, porridge
bouillon (m.)	*boo-yoN*	meat soup ; beef tea
boulette (f.)	*boo-lait*	meat ball, rissole
brochet (m.)	*bro-shai*	pike
brugnon (m.)	*br(ee)n-yoN*	nectarine
cabillaud (m.)	*kah-bee-yoh*	codfish ; fresh cod
caille (f.)	*kahy*	quail
canard (m.)	*kah-nahr*	duck
canard sauvage	*kah-nahr so-vazh*	wild duck
caneton (m.)	*kahn-toN*	duckling
cannelle (f.)	*kah-nail*	cinnamon
câpre (f.)	*kahpr*	caper
caramel (m.)	*kah-rah-mail*	burnt sugar
carottes (f.pl.)	*kah-rot*	carrots
carpe (f.)	*kahrp*	carp
carrelet (m.)	*kahr-lai*	plaice
casse croûte (m.)	*kas-kroot*	snack
cassis (m.)	*kah-see*	black currant
céleri (m.)	*sayl-ree*	celery
cerfeuil (m.)	*sair-f(ai)y*	chevril
cerise (f.)	*s'reez*	cherry
cervelas (m.)	*sair-v'lah*	saveloy
cervelle (f.) **de veau**	*sair-vail (de voh)*	(calves') brains
champignons (m.pl.)	*shaN-peen-yoN*	mushrooms
chapon (m.)	*shah-poN*	capon
charlotte (f.)	*shahr-lot*	apple charlotte ; trifle
châteaubriant (m.)	*shah-toh-bree-aN*	grilled steak
châtaigne (f.)	*shah-tainy*	chestnut
chevreuil (m.)	*shev-r(ai)y*	venison
chicorée (f.)	*shee-koh-ray*	chicory
chicorée frisée	*shee-koh-ray free-zay*	endive

chou (m.)	*shoo*	cabbage
de Bruxelles	*shoo de br(ee)-sail*	Brussels sprouts
frisé	*shoo free-zay*	kale
de Milan	*shoo de mee-laN*	Savoy cabbage
à la crème	*shoo ah lah kraim*	cream bun
choucroute (f.)	*shoo-kroot*	sauerkraut
chou-fleur (m.)	*shoo-fl(ai)r*	cauliflower
chou-rave (m.)	*shoo-rahv*	kohlrabi
ciboulette (f.)	*see-boo-lait*	chive
citron (m.)	*seet-roN*	lemon
citrouille (f.)	*seet-rooy*	pumpkin
civet (m.)	*see-vai*	stew (of venison, etc.)
civet de lièvre	*see-vai de lyaivr*	jugged hare
clou (m.) **de girofle**	*kloo de zhee-rofl*	clove
cochon de lait (m.)	*koh-shoN de lai*	sucking pig
cocotte (f.)	*koh-kot*	cooked with bacon in stew-pan
cœurs (m.pl.)	*k(ai)r*	hearts
de laitue	*de lai-t(ee)*	of lettuce
de filet	*de fee-lay*	tender loin steak
coings (m.pl.)	*kwaiN*	quince
compote (f.)	*koN-pot*	stewed fruit
concombre (m.)	*koN-koNbr*	cucumber
condiments (m.pl.)	*koN-dee-maN*	seasoning
confitures (f.pl.)	*koN-fee-t(ee)r*	preserves ; jam
conserve (f.)	*koN-sairv*	preserved food
conserves au vinaigre	*koN-sairv oh vee-naigr*	pickles
conserves en boîtes	*aN bwaht*	tinned food
bœuf de conserve	*b(ai)f de koN-sairv*	corned beef
consommé (m.)	*koN-so-may*	clear soup ; stock
coq (m.)	*kok*	cock
d'Inde	*kok daiN-d*	turkey cock
de bruyère	*kok de br(ee)-yair*	grouse
coquillage (m.)	*ko-kee-yahzh*	shell-fish
cornichon (m.)	*kor-nee-shoN*	gherkin
côtelette (f.)	*koht-lait*	cutlet ; chop
courge (f.) **à la moelle**	*koorzh ah lah mwahl*	vegetable marrow
crabe (m.)	*krahb*	crab
crème (f.)	*kraim*	cream
crème fouettée	*kraim foo-ai-tay*	whipped cream
crème au caramel	*kraim oh ka-ra-mail*	caramel custard
crêpe (f.)	*kraip*	pancake
cresson (m.)	*krai-soN*	cress
de fontaine	*de foN-tain*	watercress
crevettes (f.pl.)	*kre-vait*	shrimps

croûte (f.)	*kroot*	crust
au pot	*oh poh*	clear soup with pieces of toast
aux champignons	*oh shaN-pee-nyoN*	mushrooms on toast
cru	*kr(ee)*	raw
cuit	*kwee*	cooked
dattes (f.pl.)	*daht*	dates
daube (f.)	*dohb*	stew
dinde (f.)	*daiNd*	turkey
dindon (m.)	*daiN-doN*	turkey cock
dindonneau (m.)	*daiN-do-noh*	young turkey
échalote (f.)	*ay-shah-lot*	shallot
écrevisse (f.)	*ay-kre-vees*	(fresh-water) crayfish
endive (f.)	*aN-deev*	endive ·
épaule (f.)	*ay-pol*	shoulder
éperlan (m.)	*ay-pair-laN*	smelt
épice (f.)	*ay-pees*	spice
pain d'épice	*paiN day-pees*	gingerbread
épinard (m.)	*ay-pee-nahr*	spinach
escalope (f.)	*ais-kah-lop*	cutlet (of veal)
escargot (m.)	*ais-kahr-goh*	snail
escarole (f.)	*ais-kah-rol*	endive
esturgeon (m.)	*ais-t(ee)r-zhoN*	sturgeon
étuvé	*ay-t(ee)-vay*	stewed
faisan (m.)	*fai-zaN*	pheasant
faisandé	*fai-zaN-day*	high, gamy
farce (f.)	*fahrs*	stuffing
farci	*fahr-see*	stuffed
fève (f.)	*faiv*	bean
figues (f.pl.)	*feeg*	figs
filet (m.)	*fee-lai*	fillet
faux-filet	*foh fee-lai*	sirloin
flageolet (m.)	*flah-zho-lai*	small kidney beans
foie (m.)	*fwah*	liver
four (m.)	*foor*	oven
au four	*oh foor*	baked
petits fours	*pe-tee foor*	fancy biscuits
fraise (f.)	*fraiz*	strawberry
des bois	*fraiz day bwah*	wild strawberry
framboise (f.)	*fraN-bwahz*	raspberry
friandise (f.)	*free-aN-deez*	delicacy ; tit-bit

fricandeau (m.)	*free-kaN-doh*	stew of larded veal
fricassée (f.)	*free-kah-say*	fricassee
frit(e)	*free[t]*	fried
friture (f.)	*free-t(ee)r*	dish of small fried fish
fromage (m.)	*fro-mahzh*	cheese
de cochon d'Italie	*fro-mahzh de koh-shoN dee-tah-lee*	pork brawn
fruits (m.pl.)	*frwee*	fruit
fumé(e)	*f(ee)-may*	smoked
galantine (f.)	*gah-laN-teen*	galantine
galette (f.)	*gah-lait*	kind of flat cake
aux pommes	*gah-lait oh pom*	apple-tart
garbure (f.)	*gahr-b(ee)r*	mixed vegetable soup
gâteau (m.)	*gah-toh*	cake
gaufre (f.)	*gohfr*	waffle
gaufrette (f.)	*gof-rait*	wafer biscuit
gelée (f.)	*zhe-lay*	jelly
gelinotte (f.)	*zhe-lee-not*	hazel-hen
gibelotte (f.)	*zheeb-lot*	fricassee of hare or rabbit
gibier (m.)	*zheeb-yay*	game
gigot (m.)	*zhee-goh*	leg of mutton
gigue (f.)	*zheeg*	haunch (of venison)
glace (f.)	*glahs*	ice-cream
napolitaine	*nah-poh-lee-tain*	in layers of various flavours
pistache	*pees-tash*	pistachio nut (See also **vanille panaché**)
goujon (m.)	*goo-zhoN*	gudgeon
graisse (f.)	*grais*	fat
de rognon	*de roh-nyoN*	suet
de rôti	*roh-tee*	dripping
de porc	*por*	lard
gras, grasse	*grah, grahs*	fat, rich
gras double (m.)	*grah doobl*	tripe
grenade (f.)	*gre-nahd*	pomegranate
grillade (f.)	*gree-yahd*	grilled meat
grive (f.)	*greev*	thrush
groseille (f.)	*gro-zaiy*	
à grappes	*ah grahp*	currant
à maquereau	*ah ma-ke-roh*	gooseberry
gruau (m.)	*gr(ee)-oh*	gruel
d'avoine	*dahv-wahn*	oatmeal

hachis (m.)	*ah-shee*	minced meat
hareng (m.)	*ah-raN*	herring
bouffi	*boo-fee*	bloater
fumé	*f(ee)-may*	kipper
saur	*sohr*	red herring
haricots verts (m.pl.)	*ah-ree-koh vair*	French beans
d'Espagne	*dais-pany*	scarlet runners
beurre	*b(ai)r*	butter beans
homard (m.)	*o-mahr*	lobster
hors d'œuvre (m.)	*or-d(ai)vr*	hors-d'œuvre
huile (f.)	*(w)eel*	oil
huîtres (f.pl.)	*(w)eetr*	oysters
hure (m.)	*(ee)r*	boar's head
jambon (m.)	*zhaN-boN*	ham
jambonneau (m.)	*zhaN-bo-noh*	knuckle of ham
jardinière	*zhar-dee-nee-air*	with mixed vegetables
julienne (f.)	*zh(ee)l-yain*	clear soup with shredded vegetables
laitue (f.)	*lai-t(ee)*	lettuce
langouste (f.)	*laN-goost*	crayfish
langue (f.)	*laNg*	tongue
lapin (m.)	*lah-piN*	rabbit
lard (m.)	*lahr*	bacon
larde (f.)	*lahrd*	larded joint
légume (m.)	*lay-g(ee)m*	vegetable
légumes verts	*vair*	greens
lentilles (f.pl.)	*laN-teey*	lentils
lièvre (m.)	*lyaivr*	hare
longe (f.)	*loNzh*	loin (of veal or venison)
macaroni (m.)	*mah-kah-roh-nee*	macaroni
macédoine (f.)	*mah-say-dwahn*	hotchpotch
de fruits	*de frwee*	fruit salad
mâche (f.)	*mahsh*	corn salad
maigre	*maigr*	lean
maïs (m.)	*mah-ees*	maize
maître d'hôtel	*maitr doh-tail*	melted butter with parsley and lemon juice
mandarine (f.)	*maN-dah-reen*	tangerine
maquereau (m.)	*mahk-roh*	mackerel
margarine (f.)	*mahr-gah-reen*	margarine
mariné	*mah-ree-nay*	pickled, soused
marmelade (f.)	*mahr-me-lahd*	marmalade, stewed fruit

marrons (m.pl.)	*mah-roN*	chestnuts
matelote (f.)	*maht-lot*	fish stew
mélange (m.)	*may-laNzh*	mixture, especially of stewed fruit
melon (m.)	*me-loN*	melon
merlan (m.)	*mair-laN*	whiting
merluche (f.)	*mair-l(ee)sh*	hake, dried cod
miel (m.)	*myail*	honey
mirabelles (f.pl.)	*mee-rah-bail*	mirabelle plums
miroton (m.)	*mee-roh-toN*	stew with onion sauce
moelle (f.)	*mwahl*	marrow (of bone)
morilles (f.pl.)	*mo-reey*	morel
morue (f.)	*mo-r(ee)*	cod
moules (f.pl.)	*mool*	mussels
mousse (f.) **au chocolat**	*moos oh sho-koh-lah*	whipped chocolate cream
moutarde (f.)	*moo-tahrd*	mustard
mouton (m.)	*moo-toN*	mutton
mûres (f.pl.)	*m(ee)r*	mulberries
sauvages	*soh-vazh*	blackberries
myrtilles (f.pl.)	*meer-teey*	bilberries
navarin (m.)	*nah-vah-raiN*	mutton stew with turnips
navets (m.pl.)	*nah-vai*	turnips
de Suède	*de s(w)aid*	swedes
noisette (f.)	*nwah-zait*	hazel-nut
noix (f.)	*nwah*	nut
du Brésil	*d(ee) bray-zeel*	} Brazil nut
d'Amérique	*dah-may-reek*	
de coco	*de ko-ko*	coconut
de terre	*de tair*	ground nut
nouilles (f.pl.)	*noo-eey*	noodles
œuf (m.)	*(ai)f*	egg
œufs (m.pl.)	*(ay)*	eggs
œuf sur le plat	*(ai)f s(ee)r le plah*	fried egg
à la coque	*ah lah cok*	boiled egg
mollet	*moh-lay*	soft boiled egg
dur	*d(ee)r*	hard boiled egg
poché	*poh-shay*	poached egg
brouillé	*broo-yay*	scrambled egg
œufs au lait	*oh lai*	custard
œuf à la neige	*ah lah naizh*	floating islands
oie (f.)	*wah*	goose
oignons (m.pl.)	*on-yoN*	onions

omelette (f.)	*om-lait*	omelette
naturelle	*nah-t(ee)rel*	plain omelette
aux fines herbes	*oh fin-zairb*	savoury omelette
aux confitures	*oh koN-fee-t(ee)r*	sweet omelette
orange (f.)	*oh-raNzh*	orange
orange amère	*ah-mair*	bitter (Seville) orange
orangeat (m.)	*oh-raN-zhah*	candied orange peel
oseille (f.)	*oh-zaiy*	sorrel
pain (m.)	*paiN*	bread
grillé	*gree-yay*	toast
frais	*frai*	new bread
rassis	*rah-see*	stale bread
d'épice	*day-pees*	ginger bread
petit pain	*pe-tee paiN*	roll
panaché	*pah-nah-shay*	mixed (salad or ice-cream)
pâté (m.)	*pah-tay*	pie
pâté de cochon	*de koh-shoN*	brawn
pâté de foie gras	*de fwah grah*	goose liver paste
pâtisserie (f.)	*pah-tees-ree*	pastry
pêche (f.)	*paish*	peach
perche (f.)	*pairsh*	perch
perdreau (m.)	*pair-droh*	young partridge
perdrix (f.)	*pair-dree*	partridge
persil (m.)	*pair-see*	parsley
pet de nonne (m.)	*pai-de non*	fritter
petit suisse	*p'tee swees*	small cream cheese
pied (m.)	*pyay*	foot
pieds de cochon	*de koh-shoN*	pigs' trotters
pigeon (m.)	*poo-zhoN*	pigeon
pigeonnau (m.)	*pee-zho-noh*	young pigeon
piment (m.)	*pee-muN*	red pepper
pintade (f.)	*piN-tahd*	guinea fowl
poire (f.)	*pwahr*	pear
poireau (m.)	*pwahr-roh*	leek
pois (m.)	*pwah*	pea
petits pois	*p'-tee pwah*	green peas
purée de pois	*p(ee)-ray de pwah*	thick pea soup, pease pudding
poisson (m.)	*pwah-soN*	fish
d'eau douce	*doh-doos*	fresh-water fish
de mer	*de mair*	salt-water fish
au bleu	*oh bl(ay)*	cooked in wine
poitrine (f.)	*pwaht-reen*	breast (of veal) ; brisket (of beef)

poivre (m.)	*pwahvr*	pepper
pomme (f.)	*pom*	apple
pomme de terre	*de tair*	potato
pommes natures	*nah-t(ee)r*	boiled potatoes
pommes frites	*freet*	fried potatoes
purée de pommes	*p(ee)-ray de pom*	mashed potatoes
pomme de terre en	*pom de tair aN rob*	potatoes in their jackets
robe de chambre	*de shaNbr*	
porc (m.)	*por*	pork
pot-au-feu (m.)	*po-toh-f(ay)*	beef broth ; boiled beef with vegetables
potage (m.)	*po-tahzh*	soup
printanier	*priN-tah-nyai*	vegetable soup
potiron (m.)	*po-tee-roN*	pumpkin
pouding	{ *poo-daiN* } { *poo-ding* }	pudding
poularde (f.)	*poo-lahrd*	fattened pullet
poule (f.)	*pool*	hen, fowl
poulet (m.)	*poo-lai*	chicken
poussin (m.)	*poo-siN*	spring chicken
pré-salé (m.)	*pray sah-lay*	salt meadow mutton
prune (f.)	*pr(ee)n*	plum
de Damas	*de dah-mas*	damson
pruneau (m.)	*pr(ee)-noh*	prune
purée (f.)	*p(ee)ray*	thick sieved soup ; mash
de pois	*de pwah*	pease pudding ; thick pea soup
de pommes	*de pom*	mashed potatoes
radis (m.)	*rah-dee*	radish
ragoût (m.)	*rah-goo*	stew
raifort (m.)	*rai-for*	horseradish
raisins (m.pl.)	*rai-zaiN*	grapes
une grappe de	*(ee)n grap*	bunch of grapes
raisins		
raisins secs	*rai-ziN saik*	raisins
raisins de Corinthe	*de koh-raiNt*	dried currants
raisins de Smyrne	*de smeern*	sultanas
rata (m.) **aux choux**	*rah-tah oh shoo*	bubble and squeak
reines-claude (f.pl.)	*rain-klohd*	greengages
rémoulade (f.)	*ray-moo-lahd*	a sharp sauce
rhubarbe (f.)	*r(ee)-barb*	rhubarb
ris (m.) **de veau**	*ree de voh*	sweetbread (veal)
riz (m.)	*ree*	rice
au lait	*oh lai*	rice pudding

rognon (m.)	*ron-yon*	kidney
romaine (f.)	*ro-main*	cos lettuce
romsteck (m.)	*rom-staik*	rump steak
rôti (m.)	*roh-tee*	roast meat
roulade (f.)	*roo-lahd*	beef olive
saignant	*sain-yaN*	underdone
saindoux (m.)	*saiN-doo*	lard
salade (f.)	*sah-lahd*	salad
salade russe	*r(ee)s*	Russian salad
faire la salade	*fair lah sah-lad*	to mix the salad
salé	*sah-lay*	salted
petit salé	*pe-tee sah-lay*	pickled pork
salmis (m.)	*sahl-mee*	stew of roasted game
sandwich (m.)	*saNd-witsh*	sandwich
sanglier (m.)	*saN-glee-ay*	wild boar
sauce (f.)	*sohs*	sauce
blanche	*blaNsh*	white sauce; melted butter
piquante	*pee-kaNt*	sharp sauce
tartare	*tar-tar*	sharp mayonnaise sauce
(See also **maître d'hôtel**)		
saucisses (f.pl.)	*soh-sees*	sausages
saucisson (m.)	*soh-see-soN*	(large " dry ") sausage
sauge (f.)	*sohzh*	sage
saumon (m.)	*soh-moN*	salmon
savarin (m.)	*sah-vah-riN*	kind of cake steeped in rum
sel (m.)	*sail*	salt
selle (f.) **de mouton**	*sail de moo-toN*	saddle of mutton
semoule (f.)	*s'mool*	semolina
sole (f.)	*sol*	sole
soupe (f.)	*soop*	soup
au lait	*oh lai*	bread and milk
sucre (m.)	*s(ee)kr*	sugar
sucré	*s(ee)-kray*	sweetened
tanche (f.)	*taNsh*	tench
tarte (f.)	*tahrt*	(open) tart; flan
tartine (f.)	*tahr-teen*	slice of bread and butter
tête (f.)	*tait*	head
timbale (f.)	*tiN-bahl*	pie-dish
tomate (f.)	*to-maht*	tomato
topinambour (m.)	*to-pee-naN-boor*	Jerusalem artichoke
tortue (f.)	*tor-t(ee)*	turtle

ripe (f.)	*treep*	tripe
tripes à la mode de Caen	*ah lah mod de kaN*	braised tripe and onions
truffe (f.)	*tr(ee)f*	truffle
truite (f.)	*tr(w)eet*	trout
saumonnée	*soh-moh-nay*	salmon trout
tourte (f.)	*toort*	raised pie
tranche (f.) **napolitaine** (See **glace**)	*traNsh*	slice
turbot (m.)	*t(ee)r-boh*	turbot
vanille (f.)	*vah-neey*	vanilla
veau (m.)	*voh*	veal
ris de veau	*ree de voh*	sweetbread
veau en casserole	*aN kas-rol*	braised veal
vermicelle (m.)	*vair-mee-sail*	vermicelli
viande (f.)	*vyaNd*	meat
viandes froides	*frwahd*	cold buffet
vinaigre (m.)	*vee-naigr*	vinegar
vol-au-vent (m.)	*vo-loh-vaN*	raised pie filled with goose liver, kidneys, truffles, etc.
volaille (f.)	*vo-lahy*	poultry ; fowl

ASKING ONE'S WAY

ASKING ONE'S WAY	POUR DEMANDER SON CHEMIN	*poor d'maN-day soN sh'maiN*
Which is the way to . . . ?	Comment va-t-on à... ?	*ko-maN vah-to-nah*
The best way to . . . ?	Le meilleur chemin pour aller à... ?	*le mai-y(ai)r sh'maiN poo-rah-lay ah*
Where does this road go to?	Où mène cette route ?	*oo main sait root*
In what direction is . . . ?	Quelle est la direction pour... ?	*kai-lai la dee-raik-syoN poor*
Is this the way to . . . ?	Est-ce bien le chemin pour... ?	*ais'byiN le sh'maiN poor*
Excuse me, sir, where is the bus stop ?	Pardon, monsieur, où est l'arrêt de l'auto-bus ?	*pahr-doN miss-y(ay) oo ai lah-rai de loh-toh-b(ee)s*
Where can I find a bus for . . . ?	Où trouverai-je un autobus pour... ?	*oo troov'rai zhe (ai)N noh-toh-b(ee)s poor*
Does this bus go to . . . ?	Cet autobus va-t-il à... ?	*sai-toh-toh-b(ee)s vah-tee-lah*
In what direction must I go ?	De quel côté me faut-il aller ?	*de kail koh-tay me foh-tee-lah-lay*
Do you pass . . . ?	Est-ce que vous passez par... ?	*aisk'voo pah-say par*
Where do I have to get off ?	Où me faut-il des-cendre ?	*oo me foh-teel dais-saNdr*
Do I get out here ?	Dois-je descendre ici ?	*dwahzhe dais-saNdr ee see*
Would you be good enough to direct me to . . . ?	Pourriez-vous m'in-diquer le chemin de... ?	*poor-yay voo miN-dee-kay le sh'maiN de*
Is it far from here ?	Est-ce loin d'ici à... ?	*ais lwaiN dee-see ah*
Can I walk there ?	Est-ce que je peux y aller à pied ?	*aisk'zhe p(ay)-zee ah-lay ah pyay*
It is about twenty min-utes' walk	C'est à environ vingt minutes de marche	*sai-tah aN-vee-roN vaiN mee-n(ee)t de mahrsh*

Go straight on	**Allez tout droit**	*ah-lay too drwah*
Take the first on the right (left)	**Prenez la première à droite (gauche)**	*pre-nay lah prem-yai-rah drwaht (gohsh)*
Cross the road (square)	**Traversez la rue (place)**	*trah-vair-say lah r(ee) (plahs)*
near here	**près d'ici**	*prai dee-see*
far from here	**loin d'ici**	*lwiN dee-see*
on the right	**à droite**	*ah drwaht*
on the left	**à gauche**	*ah gohsh*
at the corner of the street	**au coin de la rue**	*oh kwiN de lah r(ee)*
tramway (street-car)	**le tramway**	*trahm-way*
underground (subway)	**le métro**	*mayt-roh*
taxi	**le taxi**	*tah-xee*
to get in	**monter**	*moN-tay*
to get out	**descendre**	*dais-saNdr*
main road	**la grand'route**	*graN-root*
side road	**un chemin de traverse**	*sh'maiN de trah vairs*
crossroads	**le carrefour**	*kahr-foor*
a fork (in the road)	**une bifurcation**	*bee-f(ee)r-kas-yoN*
a turning	**un tournant**	*toor-naN*

TRAVELLING

TRAVELLING	LES VOYAGES (m.pl.)	*vwah-yahzh*
the journey	le voyage	*vwah-yahzh*
to travel, to make a journey	voyager	*vwah-yah-zhay*
to go abroad	aller à l'étranger	*ah-lay ah-lay-traN-zhay*
to the seaside	au bord de la mer	*oh bor de lah mair*
into the country	à la campagne	*ah lah kaN-pany*
to the mountains	à la montagne	*ah lah moN-tahny*
by train	en chemin de fer	*aN sh'miN de fair*
by boat	en bateau	*aN bah-toh*
by car	en auto	*ah-noh-toh*
by air	en avion	*ah-nahv-yoN*
on foot	à pied	*ah pyay*
on a bicycle	à bicyclette	*ah bee-seek-lait*
by land	par terre	*pahr tair*
by sea	par mer	*pahr mair*
business journey	le voyage d'affaires	*le vwah-yahzh dah-fair*
pleasure (holiday) trip	le voyage d'agrément	*le vwah-yahzh dahg-ray-maN*
journey for a change of air (for health reasons)	le voyage pour rétablir la santé	*le vwah-yahzh poor ray-tahb-leer la saN-tay*
journey there	aller (m.)	*al-lay*
journey back	retour (m.)	*re-toor*
break in journey	une interruption	*aiN-tai-r(ee)ps-yoN*
round trip (circular tour)	le voyage circulaire	*le vwah-yahzh seer-k(ee)-lair*
a long journey	un grand voyage	*(ai)N graN vwah-yahzh*
trip round the world	le voyage autour du monde	*vwah-yahzh oh-toor d(ee) moNd*
route	l'itinéraire (m.)	*ee-tee-nay-rair*
passport (with visa)	le passeport (visé)	*pahs-por vee-zay*
tourist agency	une agence de voyage	*ah-zhaNs de vwah-yahzh*
time-table	un horaire	*oh-rair*
railway time-table	un indicateur des chemins de fer	*iN-dee-kah-t(ai)r day sh'miN de fair*

time of departure	heure (f.) du départ	(ai)r d(ee) day-pahr
time of arrival	heure d'arrivée	(ai)r dah-ree-vay
When is the next train (boat, plane) to . . . ?	A quelle heure part le prochain train (bateau, avion) pour... ?	ah kai-l (ai)r pahr le proh-shiN triN (bah-toh, ahv-yoN) poor
When does it arrive at . . . ?	Quand arrive-t-on à... ?	kaN-tah-reev-toN ah
booking office	le guichet	gee-shai
ticket	le billet	bee-yai
return ticket	billet d'aller et retour	bee-yai dah-lay ay re-toor
single ticket	billet simple	bee-yai siNpl
sleeping-car ticket	billet de wagon-lit	bee-yai de vah-goN-lee
reduced price	prix réduit	pree ray-d(w)ee
supplement	billet supplémentaire	bee-yai s(ee)p-lay-maN-tair
platform-ticket	billet de quai	bee-yai de kay
season ticket	carte d'abonnement	kart dah-bon'-maN
available (good) for	valable pour...	vah-lahbl poor
How long does my ticket run ?	Combien de temps mon billet est-il valable ?	koN-byiN de taN moN bee-yai ai-teel vah-lahbl
to book a seat	retenir une place	re-te-neer (ee)n plahs
corner (window) seat	un coin de fenêtre	kwaiN de f'naitr
facing the engine	face à la machine	fahs ah lah mah-sheen
with back to the engine	face à l'arrière	fahs ah lahr-yair
two seats side by side	deux places à côté	d(ay) plahs ah koh-tay
two seats opposite each other	deux places en vis-à-vis	d(ay) plah-saN vee-zah-vee
1st (2nd, 3rd) class to . . .	un billet de première (deuxième, troisième) classe pour...	(ai)N bee-yai de prem-yair (d(ay)z-yaim, trwahz-yaim) klahs poor
a berth in the sleeping car	une couchette dans un wagon-lit	(ee)n koo-shait daN-z(ai)N vah-goN lee
an upper (lower) berth	une couchette supérieure (inférieure)	(ee)n koo-shait s(ee) pair-y(ai)r (aiN-fayr-y(ai)r
a sleeping compartment	un coupé-lit	(ai)N koo-pay lee

THE LUGGAGE	LES BAGAGES	bah-gahzh
heavy luggage	les gros bagages	groh bah-gahzh
light luggage	les petits bagages	p'tee bah-gahzh
trunk	la malle	mahl
suit-case	la valise	vah-leez
travelling-bag	le sac de voyage	sakh de vwah-yahzh

hat-box	la boîte (le carton) à chapeau	*bwaht (kahr-toN) ah shah-poh*
case, chest	la caisse	*kais*
rucksack	le sac touriste	*sahk too-reest*
cushion (air-)	le coussin (à air)	*koo-siN ah air*
basket	le panier	*pahn-yay*
hamper	le panier à provisions	*pahn-yay ah proh-veez-yoN*
travelling-rug	la couverture de voyage	*koo-vair-t(ee)r de vwah-yahzh*
to do one's packing	faire ses malles	*fair say mahl*
to pack something	emballer quelque chose	*aN-bah-lay kailk shohz*
to unpack	déballer	*day-bah-lay*
to send in advance	expédier	*aiks-payd-yay*
by passenger train	par la grande vitesse	*pahr lah graNd vee-tais*
by goods train	par la petite vitesse	*pahr lah p'teet vee-tais*
to have one's luggage registered to . . .	faire enregistrer les bagages pour...	*fair aN-ray-zheest-ray lay bah-gahzh poor*
luggage office	enregistrement des bagages	*aN-re-geest-re-maN day bah-gahzh*
luggage ticket	le bulletin de bagages	*b(ee)l-tiN de bah-gahzh*
porter	le porteur	*por-t(ai)r*
fetch from the cloak-room	aller prendre à la consigne	*ah-lay praNdr ah lah koN-seeny*
take our luggage to the train (boat)	portez nos bagages au train (bateau)	*por-tay noh bah-gahzh oh traiN (bah-toh)*
to weigh	peser	*pe-zay*
overweight	excédent	*ek-say-daN*
to insure	assurer	*ah-s(ee)-ray*
to leave in the cloak-room	laisser en consigne	*lai-say aN koN-seeny*
three pieces (of luggage)	trois colis	*trwah koh-lee*

CUSTOMS	**LA DOUANE**	*doo-ahn*
to examine the luggage	visiter les bagages	*vee-zee-tay lay bah-gazh*
custom-house	la douane	*doo-ahn*
custom-house officer	le douanier	*doo-ahn-yay*
duty free	exempt de droits	*aig-zaN de drwah*
liable to duty	soumis aux droits	*soo-mee oh drwah*
to pay duty	payer les droits	*pay-yay lay drwah*
smuggling	la contrebande	*koNtr-baNd*
Have you anything to declare ?	Avez-vous quelque chose à déclarer ?	*ah-vay voo kailk shohz ah day-klah-ray*

I have nothing to declare	Je n'ai rien à déclarer	*zhe nay ryaiN ah day-klah-ray*
for personal use	des effets à mon usage	*day-zai-fay ah mo-n(ee)-zahzh*
Is there any duty to pay on this?	Cela paie-t-il des droits?	*s'lah pai-teel day drwah*
Have you any cigars?	Avez-vous des cigares?	*ah-vay voo day see-gahr*
I haven't any	Je n'en ai pas	*zhe naN-nai pah*
I have only five	J'en ai seulement cinq	*zhaN-nai s(ai)l'-maN saiNk*
How many cigars are free?	Combien de cigares peut-on entrer en franchise?	*coN-byaiN de see-gahr p(ay)-toN aN-tray aN fraN-sheez*
How much have I to pay?	Combien ai-je à payer?	*koN-byaiN aizh' ah pay-yay*
What is in there?	Qu'avez-vous là-dedans?	*kah-vay voo lah d'daN*
Only toilet things	Seulement des affaires de toilette	*s(ai)l-maN day-zah-fair de twah-lait*
These clothes have already been worn	Ces effets ont déjà été portés	*say-zay-fai oN day-zhah ay-tay por-tay*
Be careful please, these are breakable things	Faites attention s.v.p., ici il y a des choses fragiles	*fait-zah-taNs-yoN seel voo plai, ee-see eel-yah day shohz frah-zheel*
You can shut your trunks	Vous pouvez refermer vos malles	*voo poo-vay re-fer-may voh mahl*

RAILWAY   LE CHEMIN DE FER   *le sh'miN d'fair*

(See also Travelling, Luggage, Customs, Journey)

by rail	par le train	*pahr le triN*
the train starts	le train part	*letraiN pahr*
stops	s'arrête	*sah-rait*
goes through	ne s'arrête pas	*ne sah-rait-pah*
arrives	arrive	*ah-reev*
fast train	rapide	*rah-peed*
express	express	*aiks-prais*
slow train	omnibus	*om-nee-b(ee)s*
through train	direct	*dee-rekt*
passenger train	de voyageurs	*de vwah-yah-zh(ai)r*
goods train	de marchandises	*de mahr-shaN-deez*

to catch (to miss) the train	arriver pour (manquer) le train	ah-ree-vay poor (maN-kay) le traiN
to get in	monter dans le train	moN-tay daN le traiN
to get out	descendre du train	dais-saN dr d(ee) traiN
the train has no connection	le train n'a pas de correspondance	le traiN nah pah de ko-rais-poN-daNs
trains to . . .	les trains à destination de...	lay traiN ah dais-tee-nahs-yoN de
trains from . . .	les trains venant de...	lay traiN ve-naN de
station	la gare	gahr
booking-office	le guichet	gee-shay
platform-ticket	le billet de quai	bee-yai de kay
automatic machine	le distributeur	dees-tree-b(ee)-t(ai)r
waiting room	la salle d'attente	sahl dah-taNt
refreshment room	le buffet	b(ee)-fai
this way to the trains for . . .	direction de...	dee-raiks-yoN de
arrival platform	le quai d'arrivée	kai dah-ree-vay
departure platform	le quai de départ	kai de day-pahr
engine	la locomotive	loh-koh-moh-teev
luggage van	le fourgon	foor-goN
carriage	le wagon .	vah-goN
	la voiture	vwah-t(ee)r
carriage door	la portière	port-yair
sleeping-car	le wagon-lit	vah-goN-lee
dining-car	le wagon-restaurant	vah-goN res-toh-raN
station-master	le chef de gare	shaif de gahr
head-guard	le chef de train	shaif de traiN
guard	le conducteur	koN-d(ee)k-t(ai)r
compartment	le compartiment	koN-pahr-tee maN
" smokers "	" fumeurs "	f(ee)-m(ai)r
seat	une place	plahs
corner seat (next to the window)	un coin de fenêtre	kwaiN de f'naitr
corridor	le couloir	koo-lwahr
to put on the rack	mettre dans le filet	maitr daN le fee-lay
to open the window	baisser la glace	bai-say lah glahs
to raise (close) the window	remonter la glace	re-moN-tay lah glahs
to turn on the heating	ouvrir la chaleur	oov-reer lah shah-l(ai)r
to turn off the heating	fermer la chaleur	fair-may lah shah-l(ai)r
Is this the train for ... ?	Est-ce là le train pour... ?	ai se lah le traiN poor
Has the train for . . . arrived ?	Le train pour... est-il déjà là ?	le traiN poor... ai-teel day-zhah lah

The train is . . . minutes late	Le train a un retard de... minutes	le traiN ah (ai)N re-tahr de... mee-n(ee)t
Is there a through carriage to . . . in the train ?	Y a-t-il dans le train un wagon direct pour... ?	yah-teel daN le traiN (ai)N wah-goN dee-raikt poor
From which platform does the train for . . . start	De quel quai part le train pour... ?	de kel kay par le traiN poor
Where do the first (second, third) class carriages stop ?	Où s'arrêtent les voitures de première (seconde, troisième) classe ?	oo sah-rait lay vwah-t(ee)r de prem-yair (zgoNd, trwahz-yaim) klahs
Is this seat taken ?	Cette place est-elle retenue ?	sait plahs ai-tail re-te-n(ee)
Is there any room here ?	Y a-t-il encore une place ?	yah-teel aN-ko-r (ee)n plahs
There is no seat left	Il n'y a plus de place	eel nyah pl(ee) de plahs
Take your seats !	En voiture s.v.p.	aN vwah-t(ee)r seel voo plai
Do you mind if I smoke (open the window, shut the door) ?	Est-ce que vous permettez que je fume (baisse la glace, ferme la portière) ?	aisk'voo pair-mai-tay k'zhe f(ee)m (bais lah glahs, fairm lah port-yair)
How long does the train stop here ?	Combien de temps le train s'arrête-t-il ici ?	koN-byaiN de taN le traiN sah-rai-teel ee-see
What time do we arrive ?	Quand arriverons-nous ?	kaN-tah-reev'roN noo

SHIPS — LES NAVIRES (m.pl.) — nah-veer

(See also At the seaside, page 81)

liner	le paquebot	pahk-boh
Atlantic liner	le transatlantique	traNs-aht-laN-teek
steamer	le vapeur	vah-p(ai)r
cargo boat	le cargo	kahr-goh
sailing boat	le bateau à voiles	bah-toh ah vwahl
fishing boat	de pêche	de paish
motor-boat	à moteur	ah moh-t(ai)r
rowing boat	à rames	ah rahm
yacht	le yacht	ee-aht
lifeboat	le canot de sauvetage	kah-noh de sohv-tahzh
lifebelt	la ceinture de sauvetage	saiN-t(ee)r de sohv-tahzh
port	le port	por

lighthouse	le phare	*fahr*
to embark	s'embarquer	*saN-bahr-kay*
out at sea	au large	*oh lahrzh*
to land	débarquer	*day-bahr-kay*
crossing	la traversée	*trah-vair-say*
calm sea	la mer calme	*mair kahlm*
choppy sea	agitée	*ah-zhee-tay*
rough sea	mauvaise	*moh-vaiz*
high sea	grosse	*gros*
deck	le pont	*poN*
upper deck	le pont supérieur	*poN s(ee)-payr-y(ai)r*
boat deck	le pont d'embarcation	*poN daN-bahr-kahs-yoN*
promenade deck	le pont promenade	*poN prom-nahd*
prow (bow)	la proue	*proo*
stern	la poupe	*poop*
cabin	la cabine	*kah-been*
berth	la couchette	*koo-shait*
steward	le garçon (de cabine) ; le steward	*gahr-soN de kah-been*
stewardess	la femme de chambre ; la stewardess	*fahm de shaN-br*
purser	le commissaire	*ko-mee-sair*
captain	le capitaine	*kah-pee-tain*
sea sickness	le mal de mer	*mahl de mair*
basin	la cuvette	*k(ee)-vait*

FLYING	L'AVIATION	*ahv-yahs-yoN*
to fly	voler	*vo-lay*
aeroplane	un avion	*ahv-yon*
by air	par avion	*pah-rahv-yon*
aerodrome	un aérodrome	*ah-ay-roh-drom*
hydroplane	un hydravion	*ee-drahv-yoN*
parachute	le parachute	*pah-rah-sh(ee)t*
cotton wool	ouate (f.)	*waht*
air sickness	le mal de l'air	*mahl de lair*
paper bags (for air sickness)	des cornets (pour le mal de l'air)	*kor-nai*
to take off	décoller	*day-ko-lay*
to rise	monter	*moN-tay*
to fly over	survoler	*s(ee)r-vo-lay*
to land	atterrir	*ah-tai-reer*
speed	la vitesse	*vee-tais*
height	l'altitude	*ahl-tee-t(ee)d*

MOTOR-CAR   **L'AUTOMOBILE**   *oh-toh-moh-beel*

(See also Asking one's
way)

Note.—In speaking of the make of a car, one says: " Une Citroën "—
" Une Austin," etc.   Likewise when referring to one's car, one says : " Ma
voiture."

a 6-cylinder car	**une six-cylindres**	*see see-liNdr*
a 30 horse-power car	**une trente chevaux**	*traNt sh'voh*
a saloon car	**une conduite intérieure**	*koN-d(w)eet aiN-tay-ry(ai)r*
an open tourer	**une torpédo**	*tor-pay-doh*
an open car	**une voiture découverte**	*vwah-t(ee)r day-koo-vairt*
a closed car	**une voiture fermée**	*vwah-t(ee)r fair-may*
a motor-bicycle	**une motocyclette**	*moh-toh-seek-lait*
driving licence	**le permis de conduire**	*pair-mee de koN-d(w)eer*
to start up (the engine)	**mettre (le moteur) en marche**	*maitr le moh-t(ai)r aN mahrsh*
to engage the first (second, third) gear	**mettre en première (deuxième, troisième) vitesse**	*maitr aN prem-yair (d(ay)z-yaim, trwahz-yaim) vee-tais*
to engage the reverse gear	**mettre en marche arrière**	*maitr-aN mahrsh ahr-yair*
with the throttle full open ; flat out	**à plein gaz**	*ah plaiN gahz*
to hoot	**corner**	*kor-nay*
to overtake	**doubler**	*doob-lay*
to apply the brakes	**freiner**	*frai-nay*
to accelerate	**accélérer**	*ak-say-lay-ray*
to slow down	**ralentir**	*rah-laN-teer*
to park	**stationner**	*stahs-yo-nay*
PETROL STATION	**LE DÉPÔT D'ESSENCE**	*day-poh dai-saNs*
to fill up with petrol	**faire le plein d'essence**	*fair le plaiN dai-saNs*
oil	**d'huile**	*d(w)eel*
water	**d'eau**	*doh*
to change the oil	**changer l'huile**	*shaN-zhay l(w)eel*
to grease the car	**graisser la voiture**	*grai-say lah vwah-t(ee)r*
to wash the car	**laver la voiture**	*lah-vay lah vwah-t(ee)r*
to inflate the tyres	**gonfler les pneus**	*goN-flay lay pn(ay)*
a spare tin	**un bidon de secours**	*bee-doN de s'koor*

REPAIR SHOP	UN ATELIER DE RÉPARA-TION	ah-tel-yay de ray-pah-rahs-yoN
a breakdown	une panne	pahn
out of order	ne fonctionne pas	ne foNks-yon pah
broken	cassé	kah-say
burnt	brûlé	br(ee)-lay
choked	bouché	boo-shay
overheated	chauffé	shoh-fay
bent	faussé	foh-say
worn-out	usé	(ee)-zay
squeaks	grince	griNs
to repair	réparer	ray-pah-ray
to clear (a pipe), etc.	déboucher	day-boo-shay
to change	changer	shaN-zhay
to charge	charger	shar-zhay
to adjust	ajuster	ah-zh(ee)s-tay
to clean	nettoyer	nai-twah-yay
to grind	roder	roh-day
to tow in	remorquer	re-mor-kay
a repairer	un dépanneur, un ré-parateur	day-pah-n(ai)r, ray-pah-rah-t(ai)r

BODYWORK	LA CARROSSERIE	kah-ros'ree
hood	la capote	kah-pot
windscreen	le brise-vent	breez-vaN
running board	le marchepied	mahrsh-pyay
door	la portière	port-yair
seat	le siège	syaizh
window	la glace	glahs
headlight	le phare	fahr
hooter	le claxon	clah-ksoN

CHASSIS	LE CHASSIS	shah-see
back axle	le pont arrière	poN ahr-yair
front axle	l'essieu avant	les-y(ay) ah-vaN
steering gear	la direction	dee-reks-yoN
steering wheel	le volant	vo-laN
springs	les ressorts	rai-sor
bonnet	le capot	ka-poh
brakes	les freins (m.pl.)	friN
dash-board	le tablier	tahb-lee-ay
petrol tank	le réservoir d'essence	ray-zair-vwahr dai-saNs
wheel	la roue	roo
spare wheel	la roue de rechange	roo de re-shaNzh
tyre	le pneu	pn(ay)

ENGINE	LE MOTEUR	moh-t(ai)r
carburettor	le carburateur	kahr-b(ee)rah-t(ai)r
clutch	l'embrayage	aN-brai-yahzh
crankshaft	le vilebrequin	veel-bre-kaiN
ignition	l'allumage	ah-l(ee)-mahzh
magneto	la magnéto	mahn-yay-toh
battery	la batterie	baht'ree
self starter	le démarreur	day-mah-r(ai)r
starting handle	la manivelle	mah-nee-vail
sparking plug	la bougie	boo-zhee
accumulators	les accumulateurs	ah-k(ee)-m(ee)-lah-t(ai)r
valve	la soupape	soo-pahp

AT THE HOTEL

AT THE HOTEL	A L'HÔTEL	ah loh-tail
Which hotel could you recommend ?	Quel hôtel pouvez-vous me recommander ?	ke-loh-tail poo-vay voo me re-ko-maN-day
Have you any rooms vacant ?	Avez-vous des chambres libres ?	ah-vay voo day shaNbr leebr
What is the price per day (week, month) ?	Combien est-ce par jour (semaine, mois) ?	koN-byiN ais' pahr zhoor (s'main, mwah)
a single room	une chambre pour une personne	(ee)n shaNbr poor (ee)n pair-son
a double room	une chambre à deux lits	(ee)n shaNbrah d(ay) lee
a room with a private bath	une chambre avec salle de bain	(ee)n shaNbrah-vek sahl d'baiN
bedroom and sitting room	une chambre avec salon	(ee)n shaNbrah-vek sah-loN
I will take this room (these rooms)	Je prendrai cette chambre (ces chambres)	zhe praN-dray sait shaNbr (say shaNbr)
Have my luggage sent up, please	Faites monter mes bagages, s'il vous plaît	fait moN-tay may bah-gahzh seel voo plai
Have my luggage fetched from the station, please	Faites prendre mes bagages à la gare, s'il vous plaît	fait praNdr may bah-gahzh ah lah gahr seel voo plai
I should like to have a bath	Je voudrais prendre un bain	zhe vood-rai praNd-r(ai)N baiN
hall	le vestibule	ves-tee-b(ee)l
dining-room	la salle à manger	sah-lah-maN-zhay
bathroom	la salle de bain	sahl de baiN
lavatory	les cabinets	kah-bee-nay
lift	un ascenseur	ahs-saN-s(ai)r
bell	la sonnette	so-nait
key	la clef	klay
manager	le gérant	zhay-raN
porter	le portier	por-tyay
boots	le valet	vah-lay

77

chambermaid	la femme de chambre	*fahm d'shaNbr*
page boy	le chasseur	*shah-s(ai)r*
lift-boy	le liftier	*lift-yay*
the bill (for a meal)	l'addition	*ah-dees-yoN*
the (hotel) bill	la note	*not*
tip	le pourboire	*poor-bwahr*

TOWN AND COUNTRY

TOWN AND COUNTRY	LA VILLE ET LA CAMPAGNE	lah veel ay lah kaN-pany
IN TOWN	A LA VILLE	ah lah veel
a manufacturing town	une ville industrielle	veel aiN-d(ee)s-tree-ail
a commercial town	commerciale	ko-mairs-yahl
a provincial town	provinciale	proh-viNs-yahl
capital	la capitale	kah-pee-tahl
the inhabitants	les habitants	ah-bee-taN
the centre of the town	le centre de la ville	saNtr de lah veel
quarter; part of the town	le quartier [1]	kahrt-yay
suburbs	les faubourgs (m.pl.)	foh-boor
surroundings	les environs (m.pl.)	aN-vee-roN
main street	rue principale	r(ee) priN-see-pahl
busy street	fréquentée	fray-kaN-tay
quiet street	tranquille	traN-keel
narrow street	étroite	ay-trwaht
side street	latérale	lah-tay-rahl
pavement (side-walk)	le trottoir	trot-wahr
roadway	la chaussée	shoh-say
to cross the street	traverser la rue	trah-vair-say lah r(ee)
crossing	le carrefour	kahr-foor
at the corner	au coin	oh kwaiN
at the bottom of the high street	au bout de la rue principale	oh boo de lah r(ee) praiN-see-pahl
square	la place	plahs
square with garden	le square	skwahr
market	le marché	mahr-shay
botanical gardens	le jardin botanique	zhahr-daiN boh-tah-neek
zoological gardens	le jardin zoologique	zhahr-daiN zo-o-loh-zheek
bridge	le pont	poN
river	le fleuve	fl(ai)v
chapel	la chapelle	shah-pail
church	une église	ay-gleez
cathedral	la cathédrale	kah-tay-drahl
factory	la fabrique	fahb-reek

[1] In Paris : arrondissement ah-roN-dees-maN

79

museum	le musée	m(ee)-zay
exhibition	une exposition	eks-poh-zee-syoN
school	une école	ay-kol
town-hall	la mairie	mai-ree
library	la bibliothèque	bee-blee-oh-taik
castle	un château	shah-toh
policeman	un agent	ah-zhaN
police-station	le poste de police	post de po-lees
fire-brigade	les pompiers	poN-pyay
bank	la banque	baNk
hotel	un hôtel	oh-tail
cinema	le cinéma	see-nay-mah
theatre	le théâtre	tay-ahtr
embassy	une ambassade	aN-bah-sahd
tower	la tour	toor
statue	le monument	mo-n(ee)-maN
to go sight-seeing	visiter les curiosités	vee-zee-tay lay k(ee)r-yoh-zee-tay
traffic	la circulation	seer-k(ee)lahs-yoN

IN THE COUNTRY	A LA CAMPAGNE	ah lah kaN-pany
village	le village	vee-lahzh
hamlet	le hameau	ah-moh
farm	une ferme	fairm
mill	le moulin	moo-liN
forest	la forêt	fo-ray
wood	le bois	bwah
field	le champ	shaN
meadow	le pré	pray
stream	la rivière	reev-yair
brook	le ruisseau	r(w)ee-soh
tree	un arbre	ahrbr
flower	la fleur	fl(ai)r
hill	la colline	ko-leen
mountain	la montagne	moN-tahny
valley	la vallée	vah-lay
cottage	la chaumière	shohm-yair
castle	le château	shah-toh
barn	une grange	graNzh
orchard	le verger	vair-zhay
kitchen garden	le jardin potager	zhahr-daiN poh-tah-zhay
flower garden	le jardin d'agrément	zhahr-daiN dah-gray-maN
well	le puits	p(w)ee

hedge	la haie	*ai*
road	la route ; le chemin	*root ; sh'miN*
highway	la grande route	*graN-root*
local road	le chemin vicinal	*sh'miN vee-see-nahl*
footpath	le sentier	*saN-tyay*
pond	un étang	*ay-taN*
lake	le lac	*lahk*
bird	un oiseau	*wah-zoh*
fly	une mouche	*moosh*
butterfly	le papillon	*pah-pee-yoN*
ant	la fourmi	*foor-mee*
gnat	le moustique	*moos-teek*
bee	une abeille	*ah-baiy*
wasp	la guêpe	*gaip*

AT THE SEASIDE	AU BORD DE LA MER	*oh bor de lah mair*
(See also Ships)		
beach	la plage	*plahzh*
coast	la côte	*koht*
sea-bathe	un bain de mer	*baiN de mair*
to bathe	se baigner	*bain-yay*
bathing costume	le maillot de bain	*mah-yoh de baiN*
cap	le bonnet de bain	*bo-nai de baiN*
shoes	les sandales de bain	*saN-dahl de baiN*
trunks	les caleçons de bain	*kahl-soN de baiN*
wrap	le peignoir de bain	*pain-ywahr de baiN*
hut	la cabine de bain	*kah-been de baiN*
pier	la jetée	*zhe-tay*
sand	le sable	*sahbl*
breakwater	le brise-lames	*breez-lahm*
swimming	la nage	*nahzh*
to swim	nager	*nah-zhay*
to swim across	traverser à la nage	*tra-vair-say ah lah nazh*
high tide	la marée haute	*mah-ray oht*
low tide	la marée basse	*mah-ray bahs*
reef	un écueil	*ay-k(ai)y*
shingle	les galets (m.pl.)	*gah-lay*
to go fishing	aller à la pêche	*ah-lay ah lah paish*

THE POST OFFICE	LE BUREAU DE POSTE	*le b(ee)-roh de post*
Where is the nearest post-office ?	Où est le bureau de poste le plus proche ?	*oo ai le b(ee)-roh de post le pl(ee) prosh*

I want some stamps	Je désire des timbres	*zhe day-zeer day taiN-br*
What is the postage to . . . ?	Quel est l'affranchissement pour... ?	*kai-lai lah-fraN-shees-maN poor*
Three ten-franc stamps	Trois timbres de dix francs	*trwah taiNbr de dee fraN*
Five five-franc postcards	Cinq cartes postales de cinq francs	*saiN kahrt pohs-tahl de saiN fraN*
to hand in a telegram	remettre un télégramme	*re-maitr (ai)N tay-lay-grahm*
What is the charge per word ?	Quel est le tarif par mot ?	*kai-lai le tah-reef pahr moh*
reply prepaid	réponse payée	*ray-poNz pay-yay*
I want to register this letter	Je désire faire recommander cette lettre	*zhe day-zeer fair re-ko-maN-day sait laitr*
Are there any letters for me ?	Y a-t-il des lettres pour moi ?	*ee ah-teel day laitr poor mwah*
Please forward my letters to this address	Voulez-vous avoir l'obligeance de faire suivre mes lettres à cette adresse	*voo-lay voo-zahv-wahr lob-lee-zhaNs de fair sweevr may laitr ah sait-tahd-rais*
to be called for	poste restante	*pohst rais-taNt*
air-mail	par avion	*pah-rahv-yoN*
letter-box	une boîte aux lettres	*(ee)n bwah-toh laitr*
money-order	un mandat-poste	*maN-dah post*
parcel	le paquet	*pah-kai*
registered letter	une lettre recommandée	*laitr re-ko-maN-day*
printed matter	un imprimé	*iN-pree-may*
sample	échantillon	*ay-shaN-tee-yoN*
telephone	le téléphone	*tay-lay-fohn*
to telephone	téléphoner	*tay-lay-foh-nay*
telephone number	le numéro d'appel	*n(ee)-may-roh dah-pail*
I wish to 'phone to London	Je voudrais téléphoner à Londres	*zhe vood-rai tay-lay-foh-nay ah loNdr*
to take off the receiver	décrocher le récepteur	*day-kro-shay le ray-saip-t(ai)r ;*
to hang up the receiver	accrocher le récepteur	*ah-kro-shay le ray-saip-t(ai)r*
Connect me with number 6743, please	Mettez-moi en communication avec le numéro soixante-sept, quarante-trois, s'il vous plaît	*mai-tay mwah aN ko-m(ee)-nee-kahs-yoN ah-vek le n(ee)-may-roh swah-saNt-sait kah-raNt trwah seel voo plai*

The line is engaged at present	La ligne est occupée à présent	*lah leeny ai-to-k(ee)-pay ah pray-zanN*
disengaged (free) now	libre maintenant	*leebr maiNt-naN*
Are you there, Mr. B. ?	Allô! C'est vous Monsieur B. ?	*ah-loh sai voo*
This is . . . speaking	C'est... qui parle	*sai . . . kee pahrl*
I should like to speak to . . .	Je voudrais parler à...	*zhe voo-drai pahr-lay ah*

THE RESTAURANT   LE RESTAURANT   *le rais-toh-raN*

Note.—In most French restaurants a small cover charge is made ; it is called " **couvert.**''

grill room	la rôtisserie	*lah ro-tees'ree*
waiter	le garçon	*le gahr-soN*
a table for two	une table pour deux	*(ee)n tahbl poor d(ay)*
the menu	le menu ; la carte	*le me-n(ee) ; lah kahrt*
the wine-list	la carte des vins	*lah kahrt day vaiN*
table d'hôte	à prix fixe	*ah pree feex*
special dishes	les plats du jour	*lay plah d(ee) zhoor*
What will you have (next) ?	Que prenez-vous (ensuite) ?	*ke pre-nay voo (aN-sweet)*
Can you recommend this ?	Pouvez-vous recommander ceci ?	*poo-vay voo re-ko-maN-day se-see*
A knife (fork, spoon) is missing	Il me manque un couteau (une fourchette, une cuiller)	*eel me maNk (ai)N koo-toh ; (ee)n foor-shait ; (ee)n kwee-yair*
Take this away	Emportez ceci	*aN-por-tay se-see*
This is not fresh (clean)	Ceci n'est pas frais (propre)	*se-see nai pah frai (propr)*
Waiter, the bill please	Garçon, l'addition, s'il vous plaît	*gahr-soN lah-dees-yoN seel-voo plai*
You can keep the change	Gardez la monnaie	*gahr-day lah mo-nai*

FOOD   LA NOURRITURE   *noo-ree-t(ee)r*

fork	une fourchette	*(ee)n foor-shai*
knife	un couteau	*(ai)N koo-toh*
spoon	une cuiller	*(ee)n kwee-yair*
plate	une assiette	*(ee)n ahs-yait*
cruet	l'huilier (m.)	*(w)eel-yay*
dish	un plat	*(ai)N plah*
napkin	la serviette	*sair-vyait*

| a portion | une portion | *pors-yoN* |
| breakfast | le petit déjeuner | *le p'tee day-zh(ai)-nay* |

Note.—The normal French breakfast, **un café complet**, consists of a roll, butter, coffee or chocolate. It can be obtained in any café. **Un café simple,** coffee alone.

lunch	le déjeuner	*le day-zh(ai)-nay*
to have lunch	déjeuner	*day-zh(ai)-nay*
dinner	le dîner	*le dee-nay*
to dine	dîner	*dee-nay*
supper	le souper	*le soo-pay*
to have supper	souper	*soo-pay*
meal	le repas	*le re-pah*
almonds	les amandes (f.pl.)	*ah-maNd*
anchovy	l'anchois (m.)	*aN-shwah*
apple	la pomme	*pom*
apricot	l'abricot (m.)	*ah-bree-koh*
artichoke	l'artichaut (m.)	*ahr-tee-shoh*
asparagus	les asperges (f.pl.)	*ahs-pairzh*
bacon	le lard	*lahr*
banana	la banane	*bah-nahn*
bean	le haricot	*ah-ree-koh*
broad beans	les fèves	*faiv*
French beans	les haricots verts	*ah-ree-koh vair*
beef	le bœuf	*b(ai)f*
beef broth	le pot au feu	*poh-toh-f(ay)*
beef steak	le bifteck	*beef-taick*
beef tea	le bouillon	*boo-yoN*
beetroot	la betterave	*bait-rahv*
biscuit	le biscuit	*bees-kwee*
black currant	le cassis	*kah-see*
bread	le pain	*paiN*
slice of bread	la tartine	*tahr-teen*
breast	la poitrine	*pwah-treen*
broth	le bouillon	*boo-yoN*
Brussels sprouts	les choux de Bruxelles	*shoo de br(ee)-sail*
bun	la brioche	*bree-osh*
butter	le beurre	*b(ai)r*
cabbage	le chou	*shoo*
cake	le gâteau	*gah-toh*
carrot	la carotte	*kah-rot*
cauliflower	le chou-fleur	*shoo-fl(ai)r*
celery	le céleri	*sayl'ree*
cheese	le fromage	*fro-mahzh*
cherry	la cerise	*s'reez*
chestnut	le marron	*mah-roN*

chicken	le poulet	*poo-lai*
chocolate	le chocolat	*sho-koh-lah*
chop	la côtelette	*koht-lait*
crab	le crabe	*krahb*
crayfish	la langouste	*laN-goost*
cress	le cresson	*krai-soN*
cucumber	le concombre	*koN-koNbr*
cutlet ; chop	la côtelette	*koht-lait*
date	la datte	*dat*
duck	le canard	*kah-nahr*
eel	l'anguille	*aN-geey*
egg	l'œuf	*(ai)f*
	(pl. : les œufs)	pl. : *(ay)*
boiled egg	œuf à la coque	*(ai)-fah-lah cock*
fried egg	œuf sur le plat	*(ai)f s(ee)r le plah*
hard-boiled egg	œuf dur	*(ai)f d(ee)r*
poached egg	œuf poché	*(ai)f poh-shay*
scrambled egg	œuf brouillé	*(ai)f broo-yay*
fig	la figue	*feeg*
fish	le poisson	*pwah-soN*
fruit	le fruit	*le frwee*
stewed fruit	la compote	*lah koN-pot*
game	le gibier	*zheeb-yay*
grape	le raisin	*rai-zaiN*
goose	une oie	*(ee)n wah*
ham	le jambon	*zhaN-boN*
hare	le lièvre	*lyaivr*
herring	le hareng	*ah-raN*
honey	le miel	*myail*
jam	la confiture	*hoN-fee-t(ee)r*
ice-cream	la glace	*glahs*
jelly	la gelée	*zhe-lay*
kidney	le rognon	*ron-yoN*
lamb	l'agneau	*ahn-yoh*
lemon	le citron	*seet-roN*
lentils	les lentilles (f.pl.)	*laN-teey*
lettuce	la laitue	*lai-t(ee)*
liver	le foie	*fwah*
lobster	le homard	*o-mahr*
mackerel	le maquereau	*mahk-roh*
meat	la viande	*vyaNd*
melon	le melon	*me-loN*
minced meat	le hachis	*ah-shee*
milk	le lait	*lai*
mushroom	le champignon	*shaN-peen-yoN*
mussel	la moule	*mool*

mustard	la moutarde	*moo-tahrd*
mutton	le mouton	*moo-toN*
leg of mutton	le gigot	*zhee-goh*
stewed mutton with turnips	le navarin	*nah-vah-raiN*
nut (walnut)	la noix	*nwah*
(hazel)	la noisette	*nwah-zait*
oil	l'huile (f.)	*(w)eel*
onion	l'oignon	*on-yoN*
orange	l'orange (f.)	*oh-raNzh*
oyster	l'huître (f.)	*(w)eetr*
parsley	le persil	*pair-see*
paste	la pâte	*paht*
pastry	la pâtisserie	*pah-tees-ree*
peach	la pêche	*paish*
pear	la poire	*pwahr*
peas	les petits pois (m.pl.)	*p'tee pwah*
pepper	le poivre	*pwahvr*
pheasant	le faisan	*fai-zaN*
pie	le pâté	*pah-tay*
pineapple	l'ananas (m.)	*an-nah-nah*
plum	la prune	*pr(ee)n*
pork	le porc	*por*
potato	la pomme de terre	*pom d'tair*
fried potatoes	pommes frites	*pom freet*
boiled potatoes	pommes nature	*pom nah-t(ee)r*
mashed potatoes	purée de pommes	*p(ee)-ray d'pom*
poultry, wing, leg	la volaille, l'aile, la cuisse	*volahy, ail, k(w)ees*
rabbit	le lapin	*lah-paiN*
radish	le radis	*rah-dee*
raspberry	la framboise	*fraN-bwahz*
red currant	la groseille rouge	*gro-zaiy roozh*
rice	le riz	*ree*
roast beef	le rosbif	*roz-beef*
roast ; joint	le rôti	*ro-tee*
roll	le petit pain	*p'tee paiN*
crescent-shaped roll	le croissant	*krwah-saN*
rusks	des biscottes (f.pl.)	*bees-kot*
salade	la salade	*sah-lahd*
salmon	le saumon	*soh-moN*
salt	le sel	*sail*
sausage	la saucisse	*soh-sees*
sausages (dry)	les saucissons (m.pl.)	*soh-see-soN*
semolina	la semoule	*s'mool*
shrimps	les crevettes (f.pl.)	*kre-vait*

snack	un casse-croûte	*kahs-kroot*
soup	le potage, la soupe	*po-tahzh, soop*
spinach	les épinards	*ay-pee-nahr*
steak	le bifteck	*beef-taick*
stew	le ragoût	*rah-goo*
strawberry	la fraise	*fraiz*
sugar	le sucre	*s(ee)kr*
toast	du pain grillé	*paiN gree-yay*
tomato	la tomate	*to-maht*
tongue	la langue	*laNg*
trout	la truite	*tr(w)eet*
turkey	le dindon	*daiN-doN*
veal	le veau	*voh*
vegetable	le légume	*lay-g(ee)m*
vinegar	le vinaigre	*vee-naigr*
watercress	le cresson	*kre-soN*

DRINKS — LES BOISSONS — *bwah-soN*

a glass of . . .	un verre de...	*(ai)N vair de*
a cup of . . .	une tasse de...	*(ee)n tahs de*
a bottle of . . .	une bouteille de...	*(ee)n boo-taiy de*
half-bottle	une demi-bouteille	*d'mee boo-taiy*
a champagne glass	une coupe à cham-pagne	*(ee)n koo-pah shaN-pahny*
coffee	le café	*kah-fay*
black coffee	café nature	*kah-fay nah-t(ee)r*
coffee with milk	café au lait	*kah-fay oh lai*
iced coffee	café glacé	*kah-fay glah-say*
tea	le thé	*tay*
milk (cold)	le lait froid	*lai frwah*
milk (hot)	le lait chaud	*lai shoh*
cocoa	le cacao	*kah-kah-oh*
water	l'eau (f.)	*oh*
mineral waters	eaux minérales (f.pl.)	*oh mee-nay-rahl*
lemonade	la limonade	*lee-moh-nahd*
lemon squash	citron pressé	*seet-roN prai-say*
iced lemonade	citronnade glacée	*seet-ro-nahd glah-say*
orange squash	orange pressée	*oh-raNzh prai-say*
iced orangeade	orangeade glacée	*oh-raN-zhahd glah-say*
wine	du vin	*d(ee) vaiN*
white bordeaux wine	bordeaux blanc	*bor-doh-blaN*
red bordeaux wine (claret)	bordeaux rouge	*bor-doh roozh*
mulled wine	vin chaud	*vaiN shoh*

champagne	**champagne**	*shaN-pahny*
table wine	**vin ordinaire**	*vaiN or-dee-nair*
burgundy	**le bourgogne**	*boor-gony*
hock	**le vin du Rhin**	*vaiN d(ee) raiN*
port	**porto**	*por-toh*
madeira	**madère**	*mah-dair*
sherry	**Xérès**	*kay-rais*
beer (pale, dark)	**de la bière (blonde, brune)**	*byair (bloNd, br(ee)n)*
small glass of beer	**un bock**	*bock*
large glass of beer	**un demi**	*d'mee*
appetizer	**un apéritif**	*ah-pay-ree-teef*
cider	**le cidre**	*seedr*
cognac (brandy from the Cognac region)	**cognac**	*kon-yahk*
brandy	**eau de vie**	*ohd-vee*
sloe brandy	**la prunelle**	*pr(ee)-nail*
cider brandy	**le calvados**	*kahl-vahdos*
cherry brandy	**le kirsch**	*keersh*
white (grape) brandy	**le marc**	*mahr*
liqueur brandy	**la fine champagne**	*feen-shaN-pahny*
gin	**le genièvre**	*zh'nyaivr*
rum	**le rhum**	*rom*
liqueur	**la liqueur**	*lee-k(ai)r*
syrup	**le sirop**	*see-roh*

SHOPS AND SHOPPING

SHOPS AND SHOPPING	MAGASINS ET ACHATS	mah-gah-zaiN ay ah-shah
shop	le magasin	mah-gah-zaiN
departmental stores	les grands magasins	graN mah-gah-zaiN
to buy	acheter	ahsh-tay
to pay	payer	pay-yay
shoe department	le rayon de chaussures	rai-yoN de shoh-s(ee)r
shop window	la vitrine	veet-reen
showcase	la devanture	de-vaN-t(ee)r
salesman; shop assistant	le vendeur	vaN-d(ai)r
saleswoman	la vendeuse	vaN-d(ay)z
sale	la vente	vaNt
price	le prix	pree
manager	le gérant	zhay-raN
What can I do for you, Madam ?	Madame désire...	mah-dahm day-zeer
I want to buy some soap	Je désire acheter du savon	zhe day-zee-rahsh-tay d(ee) sah-voN
Have you got any razor blades ?	Avez-vous des lames ?	ah-vay voo day lahm
How many do you require ?	Combien en désirez-vous ?	koN-by(ai)-naN day-zee-ray voo
A dozen. A pair	Une douzaine. Une paire	(ee)n doo-zain; (ee)n pair
How much is it ?	Combien est-ce ?	koN-by(ai)-naise
It is too big	C'est trop grand	sai troh graN
small	petit	p'tee
thick	épais	ay-pai
thin	mince	maiNs
long	long	loN
short	court	koor
wide	large	lahrzh
narrow	étroit	ay-trwah
dear	cher	shair
Have you anything	Avez-vous quelque chose	ah-vay voo kailk shohz
bigger ?	de plus grand ?	de pl(ee) graN
smaller ?	petit ?	p'tee
dearer ?	cher ?	shair
cheaper ?	meilleur marché ?	mai-y(ai)r mahr-shay

Something in	Quelque chose en	*kailk shohz aN*
silk	soie	*swah*
wool	laine	*lain*
cotton	coton	*koh-toN*
linen	toile	*twahl*
leather	cuir	*kweer*
metal	métal	*may-iahl*
I'll take it (them)	Je le (les) prendrai	*zhe le (lay) praN-dray*
Can you change this note ?	Pouvez-vous changer ce billet ?	*poo-vay voo shaN-zhay se bee-yay*
Please send it to this address	Veuillez l'envoyer à cette adresse	*v(ai)yay laN-vwah-yay ah sai-tahd-rais*

COLOURS	LES COULEURS	*koo-l(ai)r*
black	**noir(e)**	*nwahr*
blue	**bleu(e)**	*bl(ay)*
brown	**brun(e)**	*br(ai)N ; br(ee)n*
chestnut	**marron**	*mah-roN*
cream	**crème**	*kraim*
dark	**foncé(e)**	*foN-say*
green	**vert(e)**	*vair ; vairt*
grey	**gris(e)**	*gree ; greez*
light	**clair(e)**	*klair*
mauve	**mauve**	*mohv*
pink	**rose**	*rohz*
red	**rouge**	*roozh*
white	**blanc(he)**	*blaN ; blaNsh*
yellow	**jaune**	*zhohn*

BAKER	LE BOULANGER	*le boo-laN-zhay*
baker's shop	**la boulangerie**	*lah boo-laN-zh'ree*
bread	**du pain**	*d(ee) paiN*
white bread	**blanc**	*blaN*
wholemeal (brown) bread	**bis**	*bee*
rye bread	**de seigle**	*de saigle*
new bread	**frais**	*frai*
stale bread	**rassis**	*rah-see*
a loaf	**une miche**	*meesh*
crescent-shaped rolls	**des croissants**	*krwah-saN*
rolls	**des petits pains**	*day p'tee paiN*
cake	**le gâteau**	*gah-toh*
bun	**la brioche**	*bree-osh*

BOOKSELLER	LE LIBRAIRE	le leeb-rair
bookshop	la librairie	lah leeb-rai-ree
book	le livre	le leevr
dictionary	le dictionnaire	le deek-syoh-nair
guide book	le guide	le geed
map	une carte	kahrt
hand-book	le manuel	mah-n(ee)ail

BANK	LA BANQUE	baNk
foreign exchange office	le bureau de change	b(ee)-roh de shaNzh
money	l'argent	ahr-zhaN
to change	changer	shaN-zhay
rate of exchange	le cours du change	koor d(ee) shaNzh
small change	la monnaie	mo-nai
bank note (hundred francs)	un billet (de cent francs)	bee-yai (de saN fraN)
ten-franc piece	une pièce de dix francs	pyais de dee fraN
American (Canadian) dollar	le dollar américain (canadien)	do-lahr ah-may-ree-kaiN (kah-nahd-yain)
pound (sterling)	la livre anglaise	leevr aN-glaiz
receipt	un reçu	re-s(ee)
I wish to change English (American) money	Pourrais-je changer ici de l'argent anglais (américain)	poo-rai-zhe shaN-zhay ee-see de lahr-zhaN aN-glai (ah-may-ree-kaiN)
to pay cash	payer comptant	pai-yay koN-taN
to draw money	toucher de l'argent	too-shay de lahr-zhaN
to cash a cheque	toucher un chèque	too-shay (ai)N shaik
to pay in bank notes silver	payer en billets argent	pay-yay aN bee-yai nahr-zhaN

BOOTMAKER	LE CORDONNIER	le kor-don-yay
boots	les bottines	lay bo-teen
shoes	les souliers	lay sool-yay
sandals	les sandales	lay saN-dahl
to mend	raccommoder	rah-ko-mo-day
to sole	mettre des semelles	maitr day se-mail
to heel	mettre des talons	maitr day tah-loN
high-heeled shoes	souliers à hauts talons	sool-yay ah oh tah-loN
low-heeled shoes	des souliers plats	dai sool-yay plah
polish	le cirage	see-rahzh
laces	des lacets	lah-say

BUTCHER	**LE BOUCHER**	*le boo-shay*
butcher's shop	**la boucherie**	*la boosh-ree*
meat	**la viande**	*la vyaNd*

(For kinds of meat, see Food-list on page 84.)

CHEMIST	**LE PARFUMEUR**	*le pahr-f(ee)-m(ai)r*
(See also Dispensing Chemist)		
soap	**du savon**	*d(ee) sah-voN*
razor	**un rasoir**	*uN rahz-wahr*
blade	**une lame**	*(ee)n lahm*
hair lotion	**une lotion pour les cheveux**	*lohs-yoN poor lay shv(ay)*
nail polisher	**un polissoir**	*po-lees-wahr*
nail polish	**le vernis pour les ongles**	*vair-nee poor lay-zoNgl*
shaving stick	**un savon à barbe**	*sah-voN ah barb*
lipstick	**le bâton de rouge**	*bah-toN de roozh*
face powder	**la poudre de riz**	*la poodr-de ree*
scent ; perfume	**le parfum**	*le pahr-f(ai)N*
eau de Cologne	**eau de Cologne**	*ohd'ko-lony*
cream	**la crème de beauté**	*kraim de boh-tay*
tooth brush	**une brosse à dents**	*(ee)n bro-sah daN*
tooth paste	**la pâte dentifrice**	*paht daN-tee-frees*

DISPENSING CHEMIST	**LE PHARMACIEN**	*fahr-mahs-yaiN*
aspirin	**aspirine**	*ahs-pee-reen*
Vaseline	**vaseline**	*vah-ze-leen*
iodine	**teinture d'iode**	*taiN-t(ee)r dee-ohd*
bicarbonate of soda	**du bicarbonate de soude**	*d(ee) bee-kahr-boh-naht d'sood*
castor oil	**de l'huile de ricin**	*de lweel d'ree-saiN*
cotton wool	**du coton**	*d(ee) koh-toN*
laxative	**un laxatif**	*lah-ksah-teef*
purgative	**un purgatif**	*p(ee)r-gah-teef*
palliative (pain killer)	**un anodin**	*ah-noh-daiN*
antidote	**un contre-poison**	*coNtr-pwah-zoN*
bandage	**un pansement**	*paNs-maN*
sanitary towel	**une serviette hygiénique**	*(ee)n sair-vyait eezh-yay-neek*

CONFECTIONER'S	**LA CONFISERIE**	*lah koN-feez-ree*
chocolate	**du chocolat**	*d(ee) shoh-koh-lah*
sweets	**des bonbons**	*day boN-boN*

toffee	du caramel au beurre	*kah-rah-mai-loh (b(ai)r*
crystallised fruit	des fruits glacés	*frwee glah-say*
cream chocolate	du chocolat fourré	*sho-koh-lah foo-ray*
barley sugar	du sucre d'orge	*d(ee) s(ee)kr dorzh*
sugar almond	des dragées	*drah-zhay*
DAIRY	LA CRÈMERIE	*lah kraim'ree*
	LA LAITERIE	*lah lait-ree*
milk	du lait	*d(ee) lai*
butter	du beurre	*d(ee) b(ai)r*
eggs	des œufs	*day-z(ay)*
cheese	du fromage	*d(ee) fro-mahzh*
DRAPER	UN MARCHAND DE NOU-VEAUTÉS	*mahr-shaN de noo-voh-tay*
dress materials and silk goods	étoffes et soieries	*ay-tof ay swah-ree*
woollen stuffs	des lainages (m.pl.)	*day lai-nahzh*
underclothing	la lingerie	*laiNzh'ree*
DRESSMAKER	LE COUTURIER	*koo-t(ee)r-yay*
	LA COUTURIÈRE	*koo-t(ee)r-yair*
blouse	la blouse	*blooz*
coat, cloak, mantle	un manteau	*maN-toh*
evening	un manteau de soirée	*de swah-ray*
sports	un manteau de sports	*de spor*
swagger	un trois-quarts	*trwah-kahr*
tailor made	un costume tailleur	*kos-t(ee)m tah-y(ai)r*
jacket	la jaquette	*zhah-kait*
skirt	la jupe	*zh(ee)p*
dress, frock, gown	une robe	*rob*
afternoon	d'après-midi	*dahp-rai mee-dee*
dance	de danse	*de daNs*
evening	du soir	*d(ee) swahr*
walking	de ville	*de veel*
house	d'intérieur	*d'iN-tayr-yair*
sports	de sport	*de spor*
DYERS AND CLEANERS	LA TEINTURERIE	*tiN-t(ee)-re-ree*
to clean	nettoyer	*nait-wah-yay*
to dye	teindre	*tiNdr*

FISHMONGER'S	**LA POISSONNERIE**	*lah pwah-son-ree*
fish	**un poisson**	*aiN pwah-soN*
	(See Food-list on page 84.)	

FRUITERER AND GREEN-GROCER	**LE FRUITIER**	*le frweet-yay*
fruit	**des fruits**	*day frwee*
vegetables	**des légumes**	*day lay-g(ee)m*
	(See Food-list on page 84.)	

| GROCER | **L'ÉPICIER** | *ay-pees-yay* |
| | (See list on page 84.) | |

HAIRDRESSER	**LE COIFFEUR**	*le kwah-f(ai)r*
shave, please	**la barbe, s'il vous plaît**	*lah barb seel-voo-plai*
haircut, please	**les cheveux, s'il vous plaît**	*lay shv(ay) seel-voo-plai*
not too short	**pas trop courts**	*pah troh koor*
rather short	**assez courts**	*ah-say koor*
short behind and rather long in front	**courts derrière et assez longs par devant**	*koor dair-yair ay ah-say loN pahr de-vaN*
at the sides	**aux côtés**	*oh koh-tay*
water-wave	**onduler à l'eau**	*oN-d(ee)-lay ah loh*
iron-wave	**onduler au fer**	*oN-d(ee)-lay oh fair*
permanent wave	**une ondulation indéfrisable**	*oN-d(ee)-lahs-yoN iN day-free-zahbl*
curling tongs	**le fer à friser**	*le fai-rah free-zay*

HATTER	**LE CHAPELIER**	*shah-p'lyay*
hat	**un chapeau**	*shah-poh*
felt	**un feutre**	*f(ai)tr*
bowler	**un melon**	*me-loN*
soft	**un chapeau mou**	*shah-poh moo*
straw	**un chapeau de paille**	*shah-poh de pahy*
top	**un haut de forme**	*oh d'form*
opera	**un chapeau claque**	*shah-poh klahk*
cap	**une casquette**	*kahs-kait*

| HOSIER | **LE CHEMISIER** | *she-meez-yay* |
| | (See list on page 95.) | |

JEWELLER	LE BIJOUTIER	*bee-zhoo-tyai*
precious stones	**des pierres précieuses** (f.pl.)	*pyair prays-y(ai)z*
beads	**des perles** (f.pl.)	*pairl*
bracelet	**bracelet** (m.)	*brahs-lay*
brooch	**broche** (f.)	*brosh*
ear-ring	**boucle d'oreille** (f.)	*bookl do-raiy*
necklace	**collier** (m.)	*kol-yay*
pin	**épingle** (f.)	*ay-piNgl*
ring	**bague** (f.)	*bahg*
wedding ring	**une alliance**	*ahl-yaNs*
stud	**un bouton**	*boo-toN*
golden ; silver	**en or; en argent**	*ah-nor ; ah-nahr-zhaN*
platinum	**platine** (m.)	*plah-teen*
ivory	**ivoire** (m.)	*eev-wahr*
mother-of-pearl	**nacre** (f.)	*nahkr*
pearl	**perle** (f.)	*pairl*
string of pearls	**un fil de perles**	*feel de pairl*

LAUNDRY	LA BLANCHISSERIE	*lah blaN-shees-ree*
laundry-list	**le carnet de linge**	*kahr-nayd'liNzh*
shirt	**la chemise**	*sh'meez*
vest	**le gilet de flanelle**	*zhee-lay de flah-nail*
collar	**un faux-col**	*foh-kol*
drawers, pants	**des caleçons**	*kahl-soN*
socks	**des chaussettes**	*shoh-sait*
towel	**une serviette de toilette**	*sair-vyait de twah-let*
handkerchief	**un mouchoir**	*moosh-wahr*
stockings	**les bas**	*bah*
knickers	**une culotte**	*k(ee)-lot*
skirt	**la jupe**	*zh(ee)p*
petticoat	**le jupon**	*zh(ee)-poN*
dressing-gown	**le peignoir**	*pain-ywahr*
nightdress	**une chemise de nuit**	*(ee)n shmeez d'nwee*
pyjamas	**le pyjama**	*pee-zhah-mah*
blouse ; overall	**une blouse**	*blooz*
camisole	**un cache-corset**	*kahsh-kor-sai*
chemise	**une chemise**	*sh'meez*
combinations	**une combinaison**	*koN-bee-naizoN*
corset	**le corset**	*kor-sai*
apron	**un tablier**	*tahb-lyay*
brassière	**un soutien-gorge**	*soot-yaiN gorzh*

MILLINER	LA MODISTE	moh-deest
hat	un chapeau	uN shah-po
felt	de feutre	de f(ai)tr
straw	de paille	de pahy
velvet	de velours	de ve-loor
with turned-up brim	relevé	re-le-vay
with wide brim	une capeline	kah-pe-leen
toque	une toque	(ee)n toc
beret	un béret	uN bay-ray
leghorn	une italie	(ee)n ee-tah-lee
turban	un turban	uN t(ee)r-baN
a cloche hat (with turned-down brim)	une cloche	(ee)n klosh

PASTRYCOOK	LE PÂTISSIER	pah-tees-yay
the shop, pastry	la pâtisserie	pah-tees'ree
	(See Food-list on page 84.)	

PERFUMER	LE PARFUMEUR	pahr-f(ee)-m(ai)r
the trade, shop, scents	la parfumerie	pahr-f(ee)m'ree
a cake of toilet soap	un savon de toilette	sah-voN de twah-lait
scented with violet	à la violette	ah-lah vyoh-lait
scented with eau de Cologne	à l'eau de Cologne	ah lohd'ko-lony
scented with milk of almonds	aux amandes amères	ah-zah-maN-dah-mair
eau de Cologne	l'eau de Cologne	ohd-ko-lony
lavender water	l'eau de lavande	ohd-lah-vaNd
perfume	le parfum	pahr-f(ai)N

STATIONER	LE PAPETIER	le pah-pe-tyay
stationer's	la papeterie	pah-pet-ree
pencil	un crayon	krai-yoN
pen-holder	un porte-plume	port pl(ee)m
nib	une plume	pleem
paper	du papier	pahp-yay
notepaper	du papier à lettres	pahp-yay ah laitr
pad of writing paper	un bloc de papier	blok de pahp-yay
blotting paper	du papier buvard	pahp-yay b(ee) vahr
packing paper	du papier d'emballage	pahp-yay daN bah-lahzh

toilet paper	**du papier hygiénique**	*pahp-yay ee-zhyay-neek*
typewriting-paper	**du papier machine**	*pahp-yay mah-sheen*
envelope	**une enveloppe**	*aN-v'lop*

TAILOR	**LE TAILLEUR**	*tah-y(ai)r*
made to measure	**fait sur measure**	*fai s(ee)r me-z(ee)r*
ready-made	**tout fait**	*too fai*
lounge-suit	**le complet veston**	*koN-plai vais-toN*
dinner jacket	**le smoking**	*smoh-king*
evening dress	**l'habit**	*ah-bee*
jacket	**le veston**	*vais-toN*
waistcoat	**le gilet**	*zhee-lai*
trousers	**le pantalon**	*paN-tah-loN*
overcoat	**le pardessus**	*pahr-d's(ee)*

TOBACCONIST'S	**LE BUREAU DE TABAC**	*le b(ee)-roh de tah-bah*
tobacco	**le tabac**	*tah-bah*
a box of matches	**une boîte d'allumettes**	*bwaht dah-l(ee)-mait*
cigarettes	**des cigarettes**	*see-gah-rait*
a cigar	**un cigare**	*see-gahr*
pipe	**la pipe**	*peep*
lighter	**un briquet**	*bree-kay*

WATCHMAKER	**UN HORLOGER**	*or-lo-zhay*
watch	**une montre**	*moNtr*
wrist-watch	**un bracelet-montre**	*brahs-lay-moNtr*
clock	**la pendule**	*paN-d(ee)l*
alarm-clock	**un réveil**	*ray-vaiy*
to be fast	**avancer**	*ah-vaN-say*
to be slow	**retarder**	*re-tahr-day*
to wind up	**remonter**	*re-moN-tay*

THE WEATHER

THE WEATHER	LE TEMPS	taN
What sort of weather is it ?	Quel temps fait-il ?	kail taN fai-teel
The weather is fine (bad)	Il fait beau (mauvais) temps	eel fai boh (moh-vai) taN
It is hot	Il fait chaud	eel fai shoh
cold	froid	frwah
cool	frais	frai
freezing	Il gèle	eel zhail
thawing	Il dégèle	eel day-zhail
wet	Il fait humide	eel fai (ee)-meed
foggy	du brouillard	d(ee) broo-yahr
sunny	du soleil	d(ee) so-laiy
close	lourd	loor
dull	sombre	soNbr
windy	du vent	d(ee) vaN
stormy	Il y a une tempête	eel yah (ee)n taN-pait
raining	Il pleut	eel pl(ay)
snowing	Il neige	eel naizh
thundering	Il fait de l'orage	eel fai de loh-rahzh
lightning	des éclairs	day zay-klair
a flash of lightning	un coup de foudre	koo de foodr
There is a storm in the air	Il y a un orage dans l'air	eel-yah (ai)-noh-rahzh daN lair
The sky is overcast	Le ciel est couvert	le syai-lai koo-vair
clear	clair	klair
The air is fresh	L'air est frais	lai-rai frai
stifling	étouffant	ay-too-faN
sunrise (sunset)	le lever (coucher) du soleil	le-vay [koo-shay] d(ee) so-laiy
It is moonlight	Il fait clair de lune	eel fai klair de l(ee)n
We shall have rain	Il va pleuvoir	eel vah pl(ay)-vwahr
a few drops of rain	quelques gouttes de pluie	kailk goot de pl(w)ee
a heavy shower	une averse	ah-vairs
It is pouring	Il pleut à verse	eel pl(ay)-tah-vairs
The streets are flooded	Les rues sont inondées	lay r(ee) soN-tee-noN-day

You will get wet	Vous allez être mouillé	voo-zah-lay-zaitr moo-yay
It has stopped raining	Il a cessé de pleuvoir	ee-lah sai-say de pl(ay)-vwahr
rainbow	un arc-en-ciel	ahr-kaN-syail
high temperature	une haute température	oht taN-pay-rah-t(ee)r
mean temperature	une température moyenne	taN-pay-rah-t(ee)r mwah-yain
low temperature	une température basse	taN-pay-rah-t(ee)r bahs
The barometer	Le baromètre	bah-roh-maitr
is falling	descend	dais-saN
is rising	monte	moNt
is high	est haut	ai-toh
is low	est bas	ai-bah
indicates	est au	ai-toh
variable	variable	vahr-yahbl
The thermometer	Le thermomètre	tair-moh-maitr
above zero	au-dessus de zéro	oh dai-s(ee) de zay-roh
below zero	au-dessous de zéro	oh dai-soo de zay-roh
degree	le degré	de-gray
I am cold (hot)	J'ai froid (chaud)	zhay frwah (shoh)

THE THERMOMETER

THE THERMOMETER LE THERMOMÈTRE *tair-moh-maitr*

Fahrenheit	Celsius
— 4	— 20
0	— 17,8
5	— 15
23	— 5
32 freezing point	— 0 point de congélation (zéro)
41	5
55	12,7
60	15,5
65	18,3
70	21,1
77	25
80	26,6
85	29,4
90	32,2
95	35
100	37,7
113	45
176	80
212 boiling point	100 point d'ébullition

Note.—On the Continent the Celsius (= Centigrade) scale is employed.

To turn Fahrenheit into Celsius, subtract 32 and multiply by $\frac{5}{9}$; e.g.:

$$95° \text{ F.} = (95 - 32) \times \frac{5}{9} = 35° \text{ C.}$$

To turn Celsius into Fahrenheit, multiply by $\frac{9}{5}$ and add 32; e.g.

$$-5° \text{ C.} = (-5 \times \frac{9}{5}) + 32 = 23° \text{ F.}$$

DIVISIONS OF TIME

DIVISIONS OF TIME	DIVISIONS DU TEMPS	dee-veez-yoN d(ee) taN
second	la seconde	s'goNd
minute	la minute	mee-n(ee)t
hour	une heure	(ai)r
half an hour	une demi-heure	de-mee (ai)r
quarter of an hour	un quart d'heure	kahr d(ai)r
day	le jour ; la journée [1]	zhoor ; zhoor-nay
week	la semaine ; huit jours	s'main ; (w)ee zhoor
fortnight	quinze jours	kaiNz zhoor
month	le mois	mwah
year	une année ; un an	ah-nay ; aN
century	le siècle	syaikl
dawn	la pointe du jour ; l'aube	pwiNt d(ee) zhoor; ohb
morning	le matin	mah-tiN
forenoon	la matinée	mah-tee-nay
noon	midi	mee-dee
afternoon	une après-midi	ah-prai-mee-dee
evening	le soir	swahr
dusk	le crépuscule	kray-p(ee)s-k(ee)l
night	la nuit	nwee
midnight	minuit	mee-nwee
a.m.	avant midi	ah-vaN mee-dee
p.m.	après-midi	ah-prai mee-dee
in the course of the day	dans la journée	duN lah zhoor-nay

THE DAYS OF THE WEEK	LES JOURS DE LA SEMAINE	lay zhoor de lah s'main
Monday	lundi	l(ai)N-dee
Tuesday	mardi	mahr-dee
Wednesday	mercredi	mairkr'dee
Thursday	jeudi	zh(ay)-dee
Friday	vendredi	vaNdr'dee
Saturday	samedi	sahm-dee
Sunday	dimanche	dee-maNsh

[1] Whole day in regard to work.

MONTHS	LES MOIS	*mwah*
January	**janvier**	*zhaN-vyay*
February	**février**	*fayv-ree-ay*
March	**mars**	*mahrs*
April	**avril**	*ahv-reel*
May	**mai**	*mai*
June	**juin**	*zhwaiN*
July	**juillet**	*zhwee-yay*
August	**août**	*oo*
September	**septembre**	*saip-taNbr*
October	**octobre**	*ok-tobr*
November	**novembre**	*noh-vaNbr*
December	**décembre**	*day-saNbr*

THE SEASONS	LES SAISONS	*sai-soN*
Spring	**le printemps**	*priN-taN*
Summer	**l'été** (m.)	*ay-tay*
Autumn	**l'automne** (m.)	*oh-ton*
Winter	**l'hiver** (m.)	*ee-vair*
in spring	**au printemps**	*oh praiN-taN*
in summer	**en été**	*ah-nay-tay*
in autumn	**en automne**	*ah-noh-ton*
in winter	**en hiver**	*ah-nee-vair*
What is to-day's date ?	**Quelle date sommes-nous aujourd'hui ?**	*kail daht som noo-zoh zhoor-dwee*
the 1st of January	**le premier janvier**	*prem-yay zhaN-vyay*
the 2nd of February	**le deux février**	*d(ay) fayv-ree-ay*
the 3rd of March	**le trois mars**	*trwah mahrs*

THE PAST	LE PASSÉ	*pah-say*
yesterday	**hier**	*yair*
the day before yesterday	**avant-hier**	*ah-vaNt yair*
this day last week	**il y a aujourd'hui huit jours**	*eel-yah oh-zhoor-dwee wee zhoor*
this day last year	**il y a un an**	*eel-yah (ai)naN*
an hour ago	**il y a une heure**	*eel-yah (ee)n (ai)r*
two days ago	**deux jours**	*d(ay) zhoor*
three weeks ago	**trois semaines**	*trwah s'main*
last Friday	**vendredi dernier**	*vaNdr'dee dairn-yay*
last week	**la semaine dernière**	*s'main dairn-yair*
this morning	**ce matin**	*se mah-taiN*
last night	**hier soir**	*yair swahr*
lately ; recently	**récemment**	*ray-sah-maN*
a little while ago ; just now	**tantôt ; tout à l'heure**	*taN-toh ; too-tah-l(ai)r*

THE PRESENT	LE PRÉSENT	*pray-zaN*
to-day	aujourd'hui	*oh-zhoord-wee*
now ; at present	maintenant	*maiNt-naN*
nowadays	de nos jours	*de noh zhoor*
in time	à temps	*ah taN*
It is late	Il est tard	*ee-lai tahr*
I am late	je suis en retard	*zhe swee-zaN re-tahr*
early	de bonne heure	*de bo-n(ai)r*
a little while	un petit moment	*p'tee moh-maN*
a long time	longtemps	*loN-taN*
for the present ; temporarily	provisoirement	*proh-vee-zwahr-maN*

THE FUTURE	L'AVENIR	*ahv'neer*
to-morrow	demain	*d'maiN*
the day after to-morrow	après-demain	*ah-prai d'maiN*
immediately	immédiatement	*ee-mayd-yaht-maN*
soon	bientôt	*byaiN-toh*
directly	tout de suite	*tood-sweet*
presently	tout à l'heure	*too-tah-l(ai)r*
later on	plus tard	*pl(ee) tahr*
next Monday	lundi prochain	*l(ai)N-dee pro-sh(ai)N*
next week	la semaine prochaine	*s'main pro-shain*
next year	l'année (f.) prochaine	*ah-nay pro-shain*
this afternoon	cette après-midi	*sai-tah-prai mee-dee*
this evening (to-night)	ce soir	*se swahr*
in a few days	dans quelques jours	*daN kailk zhoor*
this day week	aujourd'hui en huit	*oh-zhoord-wee aN-weet*
in a fortnight	dans une quinzaine	*daN-z(ee)n haiN-zain*
in a short while	en peu de temps	*aN p(ay) de taN*
within (after) five minutes	en (dans) cinq minutes	*aN (daN) saiN mee-n(ee)t*
a long time	longtemps	*loN-taN*
a short while	peu de temps	*p(ay) de taN*
for good	pour toujours	*poor too-zhoor*

HOW OFTEN	COMBIEN DE FOIS	*koN-byaiN de fwah*
sometimes	quelquefois	*kailk-fwah*
often	souvent	*soo-vaN*
always	toujours	*too-zhoor*
frequently	fréquemment	*fray-kah-maN*
constantly	continuellement	*koN-tee-n(ee)-ail-maN*
rarely	rarement	*rahr'maN*
never	jamais	*zhah-mai*

every day	tous les jours	*too lay zhoor*
twice a day	deux fois par jour	*d(ay) fwah pahr zhoor*
three times a week	trois fois par semaine	*trwah fwah pahr s'main*
so often	tant de fois	*taN de fwah*
now and then	de temps en temps	*de taN-zaN taN*

TIME	**L'HEURE**	*l(ai)r*
What time is it ?	Quelle heure est-il ?	*kai-l(ai)rai-teel*
It is nearly four o'clock	Il est presque quatre heures	*ee-lai praisk' kaht-r(ai)r*
It is exactly two o'clock	Il est juste deux heures	*ee-lai zh(ee)st d(ay)-z(ai)r*
It is about three o'clock	Il est environ trois heures	*ee-lai-taN-vee-roN trwah-z(ai)r*
It is five minutes past three	Il est trois heures cinq	*ee-lai trwah-z(ai)r siNk*
It is a quarter past six	Il est six heures et quart	*ee-lai see-z(ai)-ray kahr*
It is half-past seven	Il est sept heures et demie	*ee-lai sai-t(ai)r ay d'mee*
It is twenty to eight	Il est huit heures moins vingt	*ee-lai wee-t(ai)r mwaiN vaiN*
It is a quarter to ten	Il est dix heures moins le quart	*ee-lai dee-z(air) mw(ai)N le kahr*
It is five to eleven	Il est onze heures moins cinq	*ee-lai oN-z(ai)r mw(ai)N saiNk*
It is noon	Il est midi	*ee-lai mee-dee*
It is midnight	Il est minuit	*ee-lai meen-wee*
It is ten past twelve (a.m.)	Il est minuit dix	*ee-lai meen-wee dees*
It is half-past twelve (p.m.)	Il est midi et demi	*ee-lai mee-dee ay d'mee*
shortly before (after) nine	quelques minutes avant (après) neuf heures	*kailk mee-n(ee)t ah-vaN (ah-prai) n(ai)-v(ai)r*
six a.m.	six heures du matin	*see-z(ai)r d(ee) mah-taiN*
p.m.	du soir	*d(ee) swahr*
towards three p.m.	vers trois heures de l'après-midi	*vair trwah-z(ai)r de lahp-rai mee-dee*
four o'clock in the morning	quatre heures du matin	*kaht-r(ai)r d(ee) mah-t(ai)N*
eleven o'clock a.m.	onze heures du matin	*oN-z(ai)r d(ee) mah-t(ai)N*

the watch	**la montre**	*moNtr*
the clock	**l'horloge** (f.)	*or-lozh*
It is right	**Elle est à l'heure**	*ail ai-tah l(ai)r*
wrong	**n'est pas à l'heure**	*nai pah-zah l(ai)r*
fast	**Elle avance**	*ail ahvaNs*
slow	**retarde**	*re-tahrd*
It has stopped	**Elle est arrêtée**	*ai-lai-tah-rai-tay*
It has to be wound up	**Il faut la remonter**	*eel foh lah re-moN-tay*
repaired	**réparer**	*ray-pah-ray*
cleaned	**nettoyer**	*nait-wah-yay*

THE FAMILY

THE FAMILY | LA FAMILLE | *fah-meey*

THE FAMILY	LA FAMILLE	*fah-meey*
Christian name	le prénom	*pray-noN*
surname	le nom de famille	*noN de fah-meey*
the parents	les parents	*pah-raN*
relative	le parent	*pah-raN*
near relation	proche parent	*prosh pah-raN*
distant relation	parent éloigné	*pah-raN ay-lwahn-yay*
parents-in-law	les beaux-parents	*boh pah-raN*
father	le père	*pair*
father-in-law	le beau-père	*boh-pair*
mother	la mère	*mair*
mother-in-law	la belle-mère	*bail-mair*
child	un (une) enfant	*aN-faN*
son	le fils	*fees*
daughter	la fille	*feey*
son-in-law	le beau-fils	*boh-fees*
daughter-in-law	la belle-fille	*bail-feey*
brother	le frère	*frair*
sister	la sœur	*s(ai)r*
half-brother	le demi-frère	*d'mee frair*
half-sister	la demi-sœur	*d'mee s(ai)r*
grandparents	les grands-parents	*graN pah-raN*
grandfather	le grand-père	*graN-pair*
grandmother	la grand'mère	*graN-mair*
grandson	le petit-fils	*p'tee-fees*
granddaughter	la petite-fille	*p'teet-feey*
cousin (male)	le cousin	*coo-zaiN*
cousin (female)	la cousine	*coo-zeen*
uncle	l'oncle	*oN-kl*
aunt	la tante	*taNt*
nephew	le neveu	*n'v(ay)*
niece	la nièce	*nyais*
born	né	*nay*
birth	la naissance	*nai-saNs*
birthday	l'anniversaire	*ah-nee-vair-sair*
French by birth	français de naissance	*fraN-sai de nai-saNs*
baptism	le baptême	*bah-taim*
baptised	baptisé	*bah-tee-zay*

godfather	**le parrain**	*pah-raiN*
godmother	**la marraine**	*mah-rain*
baby	**le nourrisson**	*noo-ree-soN*
infant	**le petit enfant**	*p'tee-taN-faN*
(little) boy	**le petit garçon**	*p'tee gahr-soN*
(little) girl	**la petite fille**	*p'teet feey*
young man	**le jeune homme**	*zh(ai)-nom*
young woman	**la jeune fille**	*zh(ai)n-feey*
unmarried	**célibataire**	*say-lee-bah-tair*
engaged	**fiancé**	*fee-aN-say*
married	**marié**	*mahr-yay*
husband	**le mari**	*mah-ree*
wife	**la femme**	*fahm*

THE BODY

THE BODY

	LE CORPS	le kor
hair	les cheveux	sh'v(ay)
head	la tête	tait
forehead	le front	froN
face	la figure ; le visage	fee-g(ee)r ; vee-zahzh
complexion	le teint	taiN
ear	une oreille	oh-r(ai)y
eye(s)	un œil ; les yeux	(ai)y ; y(ay)
eyebrow	le sourcil	soor-see
eyelash	le cil	seel
eyelid	la paupière	poh-pyair
nose	le nez	nay
mouth	la bouche	boosh
tongue	la langue	laNg
lip	la lèvre	laivr
cheek	la joue	zhoo
skin	la peau	poh
chin	le menton	maN-toN
beard	la barbe	bahrb
moustache	la moustache	moos-tahsh
neck	le cou	koo
shoulder	une épaule	ay-poll
chest ; breast	la poitrine	pwaht-reen
heart	le cœur	k(ai)r
arm	le bras	brah
elbow	le coude	kood
stomach	l'estomac	ais-toh-mah
back	le dos	doh
hand	la main	maiN
thumb	le pouce	poos
finger	le doigt	dwah
waist	la taille	tahy
leg	la jambe	zhaNb
knee	le genou	zh'noo
foot	le pied	pyay
toes	les orteils	or-taiy
blood	le sang	saN
bald	chauve	shohv
blind	aveugle	ah-v(ai)gl

deaf	sourd	*soor*
dumb	muet	*m(ee)-ai*
crippled	estropié	*ais-troh-pyay*
humpbacked	bossu	*bo-s(ee)*
slim	mince	*maiNs*
stout	corpulent	*kor-p(ee)-laN*
young	jeune	*zh(ai)n*
old	vieux ; vieille	*vy(ay) ; vyaiy*
tall	grand	*graN*
small	petit	*p'tee*
middle sized	de taille moyenne	*de tahy mwah-yain*

He is thirty years old	Il a trente ans	*ee-lah traN-taN*
How old is she ?	Quel âge a-t-elle ?	*kai-lahzh ah-tail*
How old are you ?	Quel âge avez-vous ?	*kai-lahzh ah-vay voo*
She has a nice figure	Elle est bien faite	*ai-lai byaiN fait*
good looking	beau (m.) ; belle (f.)	*boh ; bail*
ugly	laid (m.) ; laide (f.)	*lai ; laid*
Your health ! (to some-body sneezing)	Que Dieu vous bé-nisse!	*ke dy(ay) voo bay-nees*

voice	la voix	*vwah*
to speak	parler	*pahr-lay*
to whisper	chuchoter	*sh(ee)-shoh-tay*
to call	appeler	*ahp-lay*
to shout	crier	*kree-ay*
to weep	pleurer	*pl(ai)-ray*
to sing	chanter	*shaN-tay*
to swallow	avaler	*ah-vah-lay*

HEALTH	LA SANTÉ	*saN-tay*
How are you ?	Comment allez-vous ?	*ko-maN-tah-lay voo*
How is your father ?	Comment va Mon-sieur votre père ?	*ko-maN vah miss-y(ay) votr puir*
Very well, thank you	Très bien, merci	*trai byaiN mair-see*
quite well	assez bien	*ah-say byaiN*
all right	pas trop mal	*pah troh mahl*
tolerably	passablement	*pah-sahb-le-maN*
not too well	pas trop bien	*pah troh byaiN*
You look well	Vous avez bonne mine	*voo-zah-vay bon meen*
Are you not well ?	N'allez-vous pas bien ?	*nah-lay voo pah byaiN*
What is the matter with you ?	Qu'avez-vous ?	*kah-vay voo*

ACCIDENTS AND SICKNESS	ACCIDENTS ET MALADIES	*ahk-see-daN ay mah-lah-dee*
I am ill	Je suis malade	*zhe s(w)ee mah-lahd*
I have a headache	J'ai mal à la tête	*zhay mah-lah-lah-tait*

I have toothache	J'ai mal aux dents	zhay mah-loh-daN
I have a sore throat	J'ai mal à la gorge	zhay mahl-lah-lah gorzh
I have a temperature	J'ai la fièvre	zhay lah fyaivr
I suffer from insomnia	Je souffre d'insomnie	zhe soofr daiN-som-nee
I have a cold	Je suis enrhumé	zhe s(w)ee-zaN-r(ee)-may
I have sprained my ankle	Je me suis foulé la cheville	zhem's(w)ee foo-lay lah sh'veey
I have hurt my leg	Je me suis fait mal à la jambe	zhem's(w)ee fai mah-lah-lah zhaNb
He broke his arm	Il s'est cassé le bras	eel-sai kah-say le brah
He has fainted	Il s'est évanoui	eel-sai-tay-vah-n(w)ee
Can you recommend me a good doctor ?	Pouvez-vous me recommander un bon docteur ?	poo-vay voo me re-ko-maN-day (ai)N boN dok-t(ai)r
Please send for the doctor	Ayez la bonté de faire venir le docteur	ai-yay lah boN-tay de fair v'neer le dok-t(ai)r
a pain	une douleur	doo-l(ai)r
it is bleeding	ça saigne	sah sainy
wounded	blessé	blai-say
run over	écrasé	ay-krah-zay
knocked down	renversé	raN-vair-say
bruised	meurtri	m(ai)r-tree
burnt	brûlé	br(ee)-lay
swollen	enflé	aN-flay
the doctor	le médecin ; le docteur	mayd-sa N ; dok-t(ai)r
a dressing	un pansement	paNs-maN
ambulance	une ambulance	aN-b(ee)laNs
hospital	un hôpital	oh-pee-tahl
chemist	le pharmacien	fahr-mahs-yaiN
dentist	le dentiste	daN-teest
tooth	la dent	daN
to fill	plomber	ploN-bay
to take out	arracher	ah-rah-shay
to put in a temporary dressing	plomber provisoirement	ploN-bay proh-vee-zwahr-maN

SPORT

SPORT	LE SPORT	*spor*
to play tennis (golf, etc.)	jouer au tennis (golf, etc.)	*zhoo-ay oh tai-nees (golf)*
a game of . . .	une partie de...	*(ee)n pahr-tee de*
team ; crew	une équipe	*ay-keep*
event ; race	une épreuve	*ay-pr(ai)v*
heat	une épreuve élimina- toire	*ay-pr(ai)v ay-lee-mee- nah-twahr*
semi-final	une demi-finale	*d'mee fee-nahl*
final	une finale	*fee-nahl*
half-time	mi-temps	*mee-taN*
second half	la deuxième mi-temps	*d(ay)z-yaim mee-taN*
referee	un arbitre	*ahr-beetr*
spectator	un spectateur	*spaik-tah-t(ai)r*
ground	le terrain	*tai-raiN*
handicap	un handicap	*aN-dee-kahp*
penalty	une pénalité	*pay-nah-lee-tay*
disqualify	disqualifier	*dees-kah-leef-yay*
to win (won)	gagner (gagné)	*gahn-yay*
to lose (lost)	perdre (perdu)	*pairdr ; pair-d(ee)*
to beat (beaten)	battre (battu)	*bahtr ; bah-t(ee)*
athletics	l'athlétisme (m.)	*aht-lay-teezm*
BOXING	LA BOXE	*boks*
a boxer	un boxeur	*bok-s(ai)r*
to knock out	mettre k.o.	*maitr kah.oh*
to beat on points	battre aux points	*baht-roh pw(ai)N*
fly-weight	un poids mouche	*pwah moosh*
bantam-weight	un poids coq	*pwah kok*
feather-weight	un poids plume	*pwah pl(ee)m*
light-weight	un poids léger	*pwah lay-zhay*
welter-weight	un poids welter	*pwah wel-tair*
light middle-weight	un poids mi-moyen	*pwah mee-mwah-yaiN*
middle-weight	un poids moyen	*pwah mwah-yaiN*
cruiser-weight	un poids mi-lourd	*pwah mee loor*
heavy-weight	un poids lourd	*pwah loor*
a swing	un coup balancé	*koo bah-laN-say*
a straight left	un direct du gauche	*dee-raikt d(ee) gohsh*
a right hook	un crochet du droit	*kro-shai d(ee) drwah*
a low (foul) punch	un coup bas	*koo-bah*

BOATING	LE CANOTAGE	kah-noh-tahzh
rowing boat	un canot	kah-noh
oar	une rame	rahm
sailing boat	un bateau à voiles	bah-toh ah vwahl
sail	une voile	vwahl

CYCLING	LE CYCLISME	see-kleezm
to cycle	faire de la bicyclette	fair de lah bee-seek-lait

FENCING	L'ESCRIME (f.)	ais-kreem

FISHING	LA PÊCHE	paish
angling	la pêche à la ligne	pai-shah lah leeny
to fish	pêcher	pai-shay
fishing-rod	une canne (à pêche)	kahn ah paish
line	la ligne	leeny
fish hook	un hameçon	ahm-soN
bait	l'appât (m.)	ah-pah

FOOTBALL	LE FOOTBALL	foot-bahl
association football	l'assoce	ah-sos
rugby football	le rugby	r(ee)g-b(ee)
goal	le but	b(ee)
ball	la balle	bahl
a run	une course	koors
a pass	une passe	pahs
a tackle	le plaquage	plah-kahzh
a free kick	un coup franc	koo fraN
a throw-in	une remise en jeu	re-mee-zaN zh(ay)
to be off-side	être hors jeu	aitr or zh(ay)
goal-keeper	le gardien	gahr-dyaiN
forward	un avant	ah-vaN
back	un arrière	ahr-yair
half-back	un demi gauche	d'mee gohsh
outside (wing)	un ailier	ail-yay
inside right (left)	un inter droit (gauche)	aiN-tair drwah (gohsh)
centre-forward	l'avant-centre	ah-vaN saNtr
goal post	le poteau	po-toh
free kick	le coup franc	koo fraN
three-quarter	un trois-quart	trwah-kahr
scrum	la mêlée	mai-lay
try	un essai	ai-sai
line	la ligne	leeny
kick out	un renvoi	raN-vwah

GAME SHOOTING	**LA CHASSE**	*shahs*
GOLF	**LE GOLF**	*golf*
golf-course	**un terrain de golf**	*tai-raiN de golf*
golf-club	**la canne**	*kahn*
GYMNASTICS	**LA GYMNASTIQUE**	*zheem-nahs-teek*
HUNTING	**LA CHASSE**	*shahs*
HOCKEY	**LE HOCKEY**	*o-kay*
RACING (HORSE-)	**LES COURSES DE CHEVAUX**	*koors de sh'voh*
racecourse	**un champ de course**	*shaN de koors*
a race	**une épreuve**	*ay-pr(ai)v*
a flat race	**une course plate**	*koors plaht*
an obstacle race	**une course d'obstacles**	*koors dobs-tahkl*
a steeplechase	**un steeplechase**	
the stands	**les tribunes**	*tree-b(ee)n*
the paddock	**le pesage**	*pe-zahzh*
the public enclosures	**la pelouse**	*pe-looz*
tip	**un tuyau**	*t(ee)-yoh*
to bet	**parier**	*pahr-yay*
to back . . .	**jouer...**	*zhoo-ay*
bookmaker	**un bookmaker**	*book-mak-k(ai)r*
totalisator	**le totalisateur**	*toh-tah-lee-zah-t(ai)r*
starting-point	**le départ**	*day-pahr*
finish	**l'arrivée**	*ah-ree-vay*
winner	**le gagnant**	*gahn-yaN*
RIDING	**MONTER A CHEVAL**	*moN-tay ah sh'vahl*
SHOOTING	**LE TIR**	*teer*
SKATING	**LE PATINAGE**	*pah-tee-nahzh*
to skate	**patiner**	*pah-tee-nay*
SKI-ING	**LE SKI**	*skee*
SWIMMING	**LA NATATION**	*nah-tah-syoN*
to swim	**nager**	*nah-zhay*

R.F.—8

TENNIS	LE TENNIS	*tai-nees*
tournament	le tournoi	*toor-nwah*
tennis-court	le tennis	*tai-nees*
ball	la balle	*bahl*
net	le filet	*fee-lay*
racket	la raquette	*rah-kait*
advantage	un avantage	*ah-vaN-tahzh*
forehand-drive	le coup droit	*koo drwah*
backhand	le revers	*re-vair*
service	le service	*sair-vees*
a fast service	un service canon	*sair-vees kah-noN*
deuce	égalité	*ay-gah-lee-tay*
two one	deux un	*d(ay) aiN*
two all	deux partout	*d(ay) pahr-too*
to lob	lobber	*lo-bay*
Whose advantage ?	Avantage pour qui ?	*ah-vaN-tahzh poor kee*
That's game	Ça fait jeu	*sah fai zh(ay)*
It is not up	J'ai doublé	*zhay doob-lay*

AMUSEMENTS

AMUSEMENTS	LES DISTRACTIONS	dees-traks-yoN
SHOWS	LES SPECTACLES	spaik-tahkl
theatre	le théâtre	tay-ahtr
opera	un opéra	oh-pay-rah
light opera	opéra comique	oh-pay-rah ko-meek
musical comedy	une opérette	oh-pay-rait
music hall	le théâtre des variétés	tay-ahtr day vahr-yay-tay
concert	le concert	koN-sair
cinema	le cinéma	see-nay-mah
Punch and Judy	le Guignol	geen-yol
box office	le bureau de location	b(ee)-roh de loh-kahs-yoN
to book a seat	retenir une place	re-te-neer (ee)n plahs
ticket	le billet	bee-yai
programme	le programme	proh-grahm
opera glasses	des jumelles (f.pl.) de théâtre	zh(ee)-mail de tay-ahtr
cloak-room	le vestiaire	vaist-yair
a box	une loge	lozh
stage-box	une loge d'avant-scène	dah-vaN sain
front row of boxes	les premières loges	prem-yair lozh
front box	une loge de face	de fahs
side box	une loge de côté	de koh-tay
box below dress circle	une baignoire	bain-ywahr
dress circle	fauteuils de balcon	foh-t(ai)y de bahl-koN
orchestra stalls	fauteuils d'orchestre	foh-t(ai)y dor-haistr
a seat in the stalls	un fauteuil	foh-t(ai)y
pit	le parterre	pahr-tair
balcony	le balcon	bahl-koN
gallery	l'amphithéâtre	aN-fee-tay-ahtr
a folding seat in a gang-way	un strapontin	strah-poN-tiN
upper gallery; " the gods "	le poulailler ; le para-dis	poo-lah-yay ; par-rah-dee
promenade (music hall)	le promenoir	pro-men-wahr
interval	l'entr'acte	aN-trakt

DANCING	LA DANSE	daNs
to dance	danser	daN-say
a dance	une danse ; un bal	daNs ; bahl
dance hall	un dancing ; une salle de danse	dahn-sing ; sahl de daNs
Are you fond of dancing ?	Aimez-vous la danse ?	ai-may voo lah daNs
May I have this waltz ?	Voulez-vous m'accorder cette valse ?	voo-lay voo mah-kor-day sait vahls

CASINO	LE CASINO	kah-zee-noh
gaming room	la salle de jeu	sahl de zh(ay)
cash-desk	la caisse	kais
counter	le jeton	zhe-toN
to ask in one's counters	toucher les jetons	too-shay lay zhe-toN
Put down your stakes	Faites votre jeu	fait votr zh(ay)
No more stakes can be placed	Rien ne va plus	ryaiN ne vah pl(ee)
even money chances	chance simple	shaNs saiNpl
varying odds	chance multiple	shaNs m(ee)l-teepl
all the red numbers	rouge	roozh
all the black numbers	noir	nwahr
all the even numbers	pair	pair
all the odd numbers	impair	iN-pair
all the numbers from 1 to 18	manque	maNk
all the numbers from 19 to 36	passe	pahs
the first twelve (1 to 12) numbers	première douzaine (P)	pre-myair doo-zaiN
the middle twelve numbers (13 to 24)	milieu (M)	meel-yay
the last twelve numbers (25 to 36)	dernière douzaine (D)	dairn-yair doo-zain
a single number	en plein	aN plaiN
two adjoining numbers	à cheval	ah sh'vahl
four adjoining numbers	en carré	aN kah-ray
0, 1, 2 and 3	quatre premiers	kahtr prem-yay

The above are some of the many variations possible in Roulette. There are thirty-six numbers, half of them red, half black, in addition to a " zero." " Boule " is a simpler form of Roulette, with nine numbers only, in addition to a " zero."

PASTIMES	PASSE-TEMPS (m.)	pahs-taN
Are you fond of . . . ?	Aimez-vous... ?	ai-may voo
music	la musique	m(ee)-zeek
singing	le chant	shaN
painting	la peinture	paiN-t(ee)r
drawing	le dessin	dai-saiN
sculpture	la sculpture	sk(ee)lp-t(ee)r
skating	le patinage	pah-tee-nazh
dancing	la danse	daNs
gambling	le jeu	zh(ay)
the wireless	la T.S.F. (télégra-phie sans fil)	tay-ais-aif
Do you play . . . ?	Jouez-vous... ?	zhoo-ay voo
the piano	du piano	d(ee) pee-ah-noh
the violin	du violon	d(ee) vee-oh-loN
cards	aux cartes	oh kahrt
chess	aux échecs	oh-zayh-shaik
draughts	aux dames	oh dahm
billiards	au billard	oh bee-yahr
backgammon	au jacket	oh zhah-kai
A GAME OF CHESS	UNE PARTIE D'ÉCHECS	pahr-tee day-shaik
chessboard	l'échiquier	ay-sheek-yay
king	le roi	rwah
queen	la reine	rain
knight	le cavalier	kah-vahl-yay
castle	la tour	toor
bishop	le fou	foo
pawn	le pion	py-oN
to castle	roquer	ro-kay
check (to the king)	échec (au roi)	ay-shaik (oh rwah)
checkmate	échec et mat	ay-shaik ay maht
BILLIARDS	LE BILLARD	bee-yahr
billiard-table	le billard	bee-yahr
a cue	une queue	k(ay)
a ball	une bille	bee-y

| cushions | les bandes | baNd |
| to cannon | faire un carambolage | fair (ai)N kah-raN-boh-lahzh |

CARDS	LES CARTES	kahrt
What games do you play ?	A quels jeux jouez-vous ?	ah kail zh(ay) zhoo-ay-voo
bridge	le bridge	breedzh
poker	le pocker	poh-kair
piquet	le piquet	pee-kai
whist	le whist	weest
to work out a patience	faire une patience	fair (ee)n pahs-yaNs
pack of cards	un jeu de cartes	zh(ay)-de kahrt
ace of spades	l'as de pique	ahs de peek
king of clubs	le roi de trèfle	rwah de traifl
queen of hearts	la dame de cœur	dahm de k(ai)r
knight of diamonds	le valet de carreau	vah-lay de kah-roh
ten of spades	dix de pique	dees de peek
nine of clubs	neuf de trèfle	n(ai)f de traifl
a game of bridge	une partie de bridge	pahr-tee de breedzh
(auction bridge)	(bridge aux enchères)	breedzhoh-zaN-shair
(contract bridge)	(bridge plafond)	breedzh plah-foN
to shuffle (shuffled)	battre (battu)	bahtr; bah-t(ee)
to cut	couper	koo-pay
whose deal ?	à qui de donner ?	ah kee de do-nay
whose lead ?	à qui de jouer ?	ah kee de zhoo-ay
partner	le partenaire	pahrt-nair
trump	l'atout (m.)	ah-too
no-trumps	sans-atout	saN-zah-too
trick	la levée	le-vay
to call	dire	deer
to double	doubler	doob-lay
to redouble	redoubler	re-doo-blay
to pass	passer	pah-say
suit	la couleur	koo-l(ai)r
to follow suit	jouer dans la couleur	zhoo-ay daN lah koo-l(ai)r
dummy	le mort	mor
to trump	couper	koo-pay
rubber	le robre	robr
the stakes	les enjeux	aN-zh(ay)
honours	les honneurs	o-n(ai)r
to misdeal	maldonner ; faire maldonne	mal-do-nay ; fair mal-don
to revoke	renoncer	re-noN-say

WIRELESS	LA T.S.F. (télégra-phie sans fil)	*tay-ais-aif*
wireless station	une station de T.S.F.	*stahs-yoN de tay-ais-aif*
a set	un appareil ; un poste	*ah-pah-raiy ; pohst*
(four) valve set	un appareil à (quatre) lampes	*ah-pah-raiy ah kahtr laNp*
portable set	un appareil portatif	*ah-pah-raiy por-tah-teef*
loud-speaker	le haut-parleur	*oh pahr-l(ai)r*
aerial	une antenne	*aN-tain*
valve	la lampe	*laNp*
wave length	la longueur d'onde	*loN-g(ai)r doNd*
to turn on the wireless	donner la T.S.F.	*do-nay la tay-ais-aif*
to listen in	écouter	*ay-koo-tay*
to switch on	tourner le bouton	*toor-nay le boo-toN*
to switch off	arrêter la T.S.F.	*ah-rai-tay lah tay-ais-aif*
TELEVISION	LA TÉLÉVISION	*tay-lay-veez-yoN*

APPENDIX I

SPELLING AND PRONUNCIATION

(Unless given below, same as in English.)

a, à	as in " far," but cut short.
â	as in " father," mouth wide open.
au	like the *o* of " go."
c	before *a, o, i* and before consonants, as in " cat " ; before *e, i* and *y*, like the *s* in " so."
ç	like the *s* of " so."
ch	like the *sh* of " ship."
e	at the end of a word or syllable, as a faint murmur sound, like the *a* in " ago " or the *e* of " open " ; if followed by a mute consonant at the end of a word, like the *a* in " hate " ; if followed by a sounded consonant, as in " let."
é	like the *a* in " hate."
è, ê, ei, ai, ay	like the *ai* in " pair."
eau	same as *au*
eu	like no English sound. Say *ay* with rounded lips (*ay*). When at the end of a word followed by a consonant which is not silent, like the *ir* in " sir," but with rounded lips ; e.g. " deux " is pronounced *d(ay)*, because the final *x* is silent, but " neuf " is pronounced *n(ai)f*, as the *f* is sounded (compare the paragraph below on Silent Letters).
g	before *a, o, u* and before consonants, as in " go " ; before *e* and *i*, like the *s* in " pleasure."
gn	like *ni* in " onion."
gu	like the *g* in " go."
ge	like the *s* in " pleasure."
h	is not pronounced at all.
i, î	like *ee* in " see," but very short and tense.
j	like the *s* in " pleasure."
l	as in " lamp."

o	as in "not."
ô	as in "note."
œu	same as *eu*.
oi	like *wa* in "wagon."
ou, où, oû	like *oo* in "root."
qu	like *k*.
r	pronounced as by Scottish people, even at the end of a word.
s	usually as in "so"; between vowels, as in "rose."
u	has no English counterpart. Say *ee* with your lips rounded.

NASALS

Whenever a vowel comes before *m* or *n* it becomes a nasal. There are four nasals :

an (sometimes *am*, *en* or *em*) ;

on or *om* ;

in (sometimes *im*, *ain*, *aim*, *en*, *ein* or *eim*) ;

un or *um*.

How these sounds are produced has been explained in the Introduction to French Pronunciation at the beginning of this book.

Note.—There is no nasal sound if *n* or *m* are followed by a vowel or doubled, e.g. "une" is pronounced (*ee*)*n*, "somme" = *som*, etc.

SILENT LETTERS

Consonants at the end of a word are generally silent with the exception of *c*, *f*, *l* and *r*. They are sounded, however, if followed by a word beginning with a vowel, but only if the following word is closely connected in sense with the preceding and there is no pause between the two words (compare English "ham and eggs," which sounds like one word : "hamaneggs") ; e.g. in "deux portes" the *x* is silent, because the following letter is a consonant, but "deux amis" is pronounced *d*(*ay*)-*zah-mee*, because "deux" is followed by a vowel, the *x* is sounded and the two words are joined together.

Nouns in " teur " change this ending into " trice " : un acteur (actor), une actrice ; un spectateur (spectator), une spectatrice, etc.

Nouns ending in " en," " on," " t " double the final consonant besides adding " e " mute : le citoyen (citizen), la citoyenne ; le lion, la lionne ; le chat (cat), la chatte.

2. *Nouns ending in " tion "*

la nation, nation   la révolution, revolution

3. *Most nouns ending in " e "*

la robe, dress   la sortie, exit   une année, year

Exceptions :

le crime, crime	le doute, doubt	le fleuve, river
le livre, book	le monde, world	le nombre, number
un ange, angel	le beurre, butter	le légume, vegetable
le peigne, comb	le rêve, dream	le siège, seat
le sucre, sugar	le verre, glass	le timbre, stamp

WORDS SPELLED ALIKE BUT OF DIFFERENT GENDER

le livre, book	la livre, pound
le manche, handle	la manche, sleeve
le page, page-boy	la page, page (of a book)
le poêle, stove	la poêle, frying pan
le poste, situation, post	la poste, post-office
le tour, trick, turn	la tour, tower
le voile, veil	la voile, sail

APPENDIX III

FALSE FRIENDS

The Deceptive Similarity of Some Common Words

MANY thousands of the most common English words are of French origin, or have been taken from the same Greek or Latin source. This similarity is not entirely without pitfalls. A number of words that are spelled the same, or similarly, have different meanings in the two languages. In the vocabulary which follows, some of the " deceptive words " or " false friends " are given.

large does not mean large, but broad or wide.
laboureur is not a labourer, but a farm worker.
blesser is to wound (to bless = *bénir*).
crayon = pencil (English crayon = *un crayon de pastel*).
demander = to ask for (to demand = *exiger*).
défendre means not only to defend, but also to forbid.
le front = forehead (the front = *la face, le devant*).
la fabrique = factory (the fabric = *le tissu*).
grand = big, tall, high, great (English grand = *splendide, noble*).
un habit = coat (English habit = *une habitude, une coutume*).
altérer means to alter, but only for the worse ; otherwise it must be rendered by *changer, modifier* or *retoucher*.
actuellement = at present (actually = *réellement*).
le lard = bacon (English lard = *le saindoux*).
la lecture = reading ; la salle de lecture = reading room (English lecture = *une conférence*).
la librairie = bookshop (the library = *la bibliothèque*).
le magasin = shop (English magazine = *une revue*).
la monnaie = change (money = *l'argent*).
la prune = plum (English prune = *le pruneau*).
la rente = income, annuity, dividends (English rent = *le loyer*).
rude = rough, harsh (English rude = *grossier*).

sensible = sensitive (English sensible = *sensé*).

le corps is not only the corpse, but the body of a living person as well.

une nouvelle (besides meaning a piece of news) is a tale or a story (English novel = *un roman*).

une occasion (besides meaning an opportunity) is a bargain.

THE NEXT STEP

To students in London we specially recommend the new method of learning languages through talking films. Just as a child learns to speak without a teacher when surrounded by people who speak the language, the condition under which a child learns can be recreated through suitable teaching films. To enable students to understand every word of the films, scripts of the dialogues are provided. These are explained and translated to the students, so that they can understand every word in the films. Enquiries should be addressed to the Secretary, Language Film Classes and Publications, 13, Suffolk Street, Haymarket, London, S.W.1.

BN Publishing

Improving People's Life

www.bnpublishing.net